Behind These Eyes

Whooptolly Chronicles Book One

JARRETT BETTS

PublishAmerica
Baltimore

First printing

ISBN: 1-60703-455-7
PUBLISHED BY PUBLISHAMERICA, LLLP
www.publishamerica.com
Baltimore

Printed in the United States of America

This book is dedicated to my mother.
This book is dedicated to my father.
This book is dedicated to my little sisters.
This book is dedicated to my big sister.
This book is dedicated to my aunts and uncles and cousins.
This book is dedicated to all my close friends.
This book is dedicated to all those people who would grace its pages with their eyes, to travel with me throughout the unlimited world of imagination, and ponder the words "what if?"
This book is dedicated to myself- to all the struggle and hardship of this life, as well as the pleasant, laughter-filled times I've spent with those that I love.
But most of all, my literary friends, this book is dedicated to YOU. Without you my work is nothing, and will be nothing but words on paper. You give it life, you give it meaning; you will make it as you will, in the confines of your own imagination, and if it becomes something that people talk about in the years to come, it will have been because of you.
Thank you for your time and peace out.

~Jarrett

Nostalgia

"You feel the urge, don't you?" The voice from the backseat was undoubtedly Seth's, one look in the rear-view confirmed it by revealing his pale, ever-grinning skin-and-bone face. His eyes were always bright with the anticipation of fulfillment; the dark fulfillment that only select few ever feel the urge to embrace.

"The urge is always there, like the body's thirst for water." Peter said, thinking: *Why do red lights always last so long when you're in a damn hurry?* He drummed his fingers impatiently on the steering wheel, trying with all his might to *will* the light into action. It didn't help change the light, but it helped him feel like he was doing *something.*

Seth's smile faltered a bit. "Only for you. For me the urge is like the need to breathe." He held his eyes on the mirror for another few seconds, then turned his attention to the passing city. His gaze suddenly snapped to a nearby building, and he nearly jumped out of his seat with manic excitement. "Look, Big-5! I love that place! We can get a shotgun and some shells, then use it on the employees! Hatchets, combat knives, fishing lures, power tools..." In his childish delight he grinned a grin that seemed too large for his face; a Cheshire-Cat grin that was a little disturbing. "Oh can we? *Please*?"

Peter shook his head, and the light miraculously turned green, causing him to wonder for a split second whether or not he emitted some sort of electrical impulse that changed the frequency running the traffic light. "It's too risky. Besides, mass-murder in the sunlight always makes for a bad day." The last time they tried *that,* they spent twenty-three hours on the run from the Hurkens Police department, twelve of those hours spent in the deep recesses of a three-foot drainage pipe that ran under marker 131S of Highway 119.

Seth's gaze turned thoughtful. "That's true..." He stared longingly at the store as it passed behind them. "But it would be ever so much *fun.*" Seth was always an impulse-killer; controlled by primal emotion and swept along by the waves of his madness, he killed whenever he wanted, however he wanted, and *whomever* he wanted with absolutely no thought whatsoever for the inevitable consequences that followed. Peter on the other hand, was a thinker; he planned every possible move with an undeniable clarity, carefully constructing each series of events that would lead to the death of his victim, with the least amount of endangerment to himself by either bodily harm or imprisonment by the law.

Peter laughed in agreement. "I'll tell you what, you just chillax until the sun goes down, and tonight we'll get that shotgun." Before Seth could celebrate he added, "But no sporting good stores, those poor bastards have a hard enough life dealing with customer 'roid rage. We'll hit a bar instead."

Seth was equally satisfied with the change of location, due to the impending promise of murderous activities. "Yeah! Fuck those alcoholic bottom-feeders!" He shouted gleefully, drumming his hands on the back of Peter's seat. Then an odd look came upon his face, as if he had suddenly asked himself a question along the lines of *'did I remember to turn off the stove when I left the house this morning?'* or *'didn't I see that man on America's Most Wanted last night?'* "Hey, your daddy was an alcoholic too, huh?"

"Shut up, Seth." Peter replied in a cold voice.

There was no need to think about *him*, all that noise was in the past

(water under the bridge)

and he would be damned if he was going to let that old man get to him again after all these years. The past was buried*(not buried,* burned)

and what's done is done. *So just let it go, stop thinking about it.* But he couldn't. Not now, now that the faucet of his memories had been opened with a rusty creak, spilling forth the putrid fluid of selectively forgotten events from his youth.

Seth said nothing else as Peter drove along Lilac Avenue and merged onto Memory Lane (but in the land of the Whooptolly, it was known as *Lunacy* Lane); when Peter looked into the mirror, he was gone.

- -

The Sea

"You got to look hard, Petey." Amos said, looking into the little square mirror that was the front of their bathroom medicine cabinet. "Look so *hard* into your eyes, and you'll see it: the sea, the maddened sea." He spoke of it as if it were a treasure, or a priceless relic of a civilization now forever lost. "It is vast and unyielding and cruel, but if your vessel is strong enough you can sail it. There is no ferryman to whisk you across this, oh no. Not even for your soul, son." Amos paused to drain the last of his pocket-bottle of Old Crow, then said, half to himself, "If I can sail this to the end, I'll see her again."

Petey, just two months away from his fifth birthday, stood on the little step that Amos had built for him, peering into the mirror next to his father, trying desperately to see what he was so lucidly talking about. "I don't see anything, daddy. I don't see the ocean."

Petey didn't see it coming, but was immediately aware of the hand slapping him as it lifted him off the step, knocking him to the floor. A bright flash of white (resulting from his head's impact on the ceramic tile) caused him to become momentarily blind, and for a frightening few seconds, Petey feared that he would be in the white forever, blind for the rest of his days and unable to escape.

"That's because you killed her you little fuck!" Amos was standing over him now, spraying spittle, bloodshot eyes bulging ever so widely. His thinning, gray hair hung down in strings, adding the totality of appearance to his seething madness. "And you'll *never* see your mother because you *killed* her! You waited too long to be born and grew too big and the doctors couldn't save her! It's-all-your-fault-she's-dead-you-little-motherfucker! YOUR FAULT!!" Amos reached his crescendo with a howl that was nearly devoid of all humanity. "LET'S PLAY BOY!" And he started smashing Petey with his fists over and over.

In a moment of savage beating, Petey looked into his father's eyes (his father was now completely *gone,*) and he saw *it.* Swimming behind those feverish eyes he saw waves of despair; an ocean of insanity. *The maddened sea.* He saw in Amos what he did not see in himself, and knew that it was a powerful thing to have the sea behind your eyes *if* you could control it.

He lay there and took his beating (which would land him in I.C.U. all the way through the time until his birthday) with one thought burning like a supernova in his mind: one day he would be every bit as powerful as his father, with those eyes of madness.

- -

Journal Entry: Sunday, Dec. 2nd

I can't look in the mirror anymore because I see that other world that the Whooptollies have shown me, through the tear in the fabric of what separates us from the infinities beyond. It is a vast sea of lunacy that beckons those who would come forth and gaze upon its maddening waters, to be held for the span of an eternity. The veil is ever so thin, fragile, and once you look through to the waters beyond you can never be the same. I am not the same, I am more than I ever wanted to be, consumed by madness ever so steadily, speaking to those who should not be here, not knowing if the reality is substantial or ethereal. I catch myself gazing at the waters that haunt me so, finding it ever so difficult to return from the hell that I warmly embrace.

What makes it so terrible is not the madness itself, but the times of sanity that are between the glimpses, and the fact that they appear less and less often. The loss of touch is not so bad, like a waking dream, but the inevitability of complete and utter insanity is a truth that I don't want to consider, yet I can't stop thinking about it.

I find myself staring into space (but not just space) for several minutes at a time; my thoughts are haunted by waking dreams and I can see the crack, opening in my walls of sanity, filling me with wonder and awe, for is not the person who questions their sanity a rational being? Is it possible to be both sane and less-than-sane?

I find myself thinking about a world within a world; something just next door, separated by a sheer membrane that is sometimes broken, or torn, so that one can see through to the other side. And what is seen through that tearing is…

The sea. But it's much more than that. You may not understand. The point is that it is there, *in this glimpse, as well as something dark and forbidding. A despair that must surely be known to cancer patients, in the dead of night, as they stare down into their empty tumblers; when the meds are all gone but the pain is still there and there are so many hours until morning.* So long until morning. *That sort of despair lurks within the shadows of the divide, like something vile that is seen in the mirror after dusk, when all the lights are off and the Whooptollies have come to have their say; like what can be seen in the murky depths of a shot glass when tilted just right way as you sit, swallowing your poison. Of that* other *world I am awed and fearful and overjoyed all at once; I can't help but stare at that pool of lunacy as it pulls me down and down and down…*

Then I am here once again, in my fold of reality, once again sane (but also capable of being less-than-sane). Oh, when I glimpse the pool, I glimpse my own madness.

- -

Hammer-Time

Jeremy sat in the center of the couch he had bought at the Thrifty Loft (at a price reduction of 75%, due to a urine stain caused by an elderly man with Alzheimer's) rolling his joint; each time that he came across a stray seed or stem, he would extract the pesky object and flick it onto the carpet. "I'm telling you Pete, there *is* no Heaven or Hell, that's just shit that some wackos cooked up to empower their little church club and trick gullible people into living their lives like they're *told* to." He twisted the ends of, then lit his joint. "Just picture it for a second: they want us to believe that there is an all-powerful, invisible deity that lives in the sky. *And,* if we don't live exactly like this deity says, then we get sent straight to the fabled frying pan." He shook his head, then took another long draw. "I'm telling you, the only believable part of their story is that this deity believes us to be so incapable of honoring spoken agreement, he made us an instruction manual!" He finished with a cloud of smoke, bursting into mated laugh and cough.

(*Tell him.*)

"You know, it contradicts itself." Peter said.

Jeremy's glazed eyes snapped back from the other-world of his rant. "What?"

"The Bible. It contradicts itself." Peter enunciated slowly this time, as if speaking to a foreigner just learning the language.

"Oh yeah?" Took the bait.

Peter nodded. "Exodus, chapter twenty, verse thirteen: 'thou shalt not kill.' Yet in Ecclesiastes, chapter three, it says that there is a time for everything, including a time to kill. Then, in Leviticus, it says to kill all sorts of people: idolaters, adulterers, gays, magicians, and those who curse their parents. That's just naming a few."

Jeremy raised his hands in the traditional stop gesture. "Whoa now, hold the boat Gilligan. Two part-er: One, when did *you* become, and I say this with the utmost respect, such the outcast to modern society that you quote random shit from the Bible; and two, *does* the Bible really say it's okay to ice the fags?" Jeremy, like many other times in his life, gave new meaning to the phrase 'dumb-founded.'

Peter kept his face expressionless. "Leviticus, chapter twenty, verse thirteen: 'if a man also lie with mankind, as he lieth with a woman, both of them have committed an abomination; they shall surely be put to death.' And I *believe* I became an outcast to society about the same time I started hanging out with *your* dumb-ass."

Jeremy laughed, coughing on smoke at the same time. "That's crazy, man. I guess I'll never have to feel bad calling anyone a pillow-biter again."

Peter broke down and laughed finally. "Or butt-pirate."

More laughter. Peter looked at his watch, and realized that it was almost eight-thirty. "I got to jet, man."

"Where you off to?"

Peter started to check his list of worthy alibis, but figured that telling this pothead the truth wouldn't hurt any.

"I've got a date." He left out the part where it involved killing a waitress.

Jeremy raised his eyebrows. "Sweet." Then he paused, a smile upon his face. "Girl, right?"

"Yeah, fuck-head, a girl."

"Do-able?"

"*Dead* gorgeous."

"Right on. Smack her ass for me, will ya?" He said casually, then turned back to the T.V.

"Affirmative."

After commandeering a black Chevy Blazer, Peter drove to the nearby city of Blakefield (with Seth riding in customary backseat driver's-side position) and stopped in the parking lot of a small hardware store. Once inside, he picked out a box-cutter, a package of a dozen blades, a black & decker power drill, and some long zip ties. The cashier gave the zip ties a second glance, but apparently wasn't in the mood to say anything, for he only announced the total. Peter handed the kid a hundred-dollar bill, took his change, then turned to leave.

"Petey." Seth's voice whispering in his ear caused him to stop just short of the door. There was only one person in the world that ever called him Petey, and that was-

"Let's play, Petey."

Peter slowly turned his gaze back to the cashier, hearing waves echoing in his mind, and with a smile slowly spreading across his face. He briskly walked back to the counter, setting the purchased items down. "I'm sorry, I totally forgot." He reached into the paper bag and pulled out the box-cutter, showing it to the cashier. "Could you possibly show me how to load this?" He flashed a smile worthy of an award.

The cashier gave him an easily read look, one of those snotty, teenage, *'eat-shit-and-die'* looks. "There's already one in it." Then under his breath, barely perceptible, "Retard."

Peter's smile faded, and a jet of acidic rage shot into his chest. (Sure the little shit was about to die, but was it necessary to be so *rude?)* He slid the unseen blade into business position, and the fluorescent lighting reflected off it beautifully. He watched, transfixed, for a seemingly endless amount of time, then looked up at the cashier. "Oh. How convenient." *(Let's play, Petey.)* He allowed his smile to return to full beaming volume.

"Uhh, yeah. Whatever."

The cashier. The rude, drugged-out, I'm-so-damn-happy-to-be-here cashier, with his foot-long chain and his ass hanging out of his jeans. The little prick would probably be happier slinging crack to kinder gardeners *(play)* than this respectable, nine to five-

(*LET'S PLAY BOY!)*

Seth's voice was undeniable.

"What the fuck's wrong with you?" The cashier

was looking at Peter with an expression that was both irritated and alarmed at the same time.

Peter realized that he had been holding his breath the entire time of this break; he released it, took in a few quick puffs of air, then exploded into motion. He swung the box-cutter in a wide, lightning-quick arc, catching the late-reacting cashier in the jugular vein, and sending a glittering spray of blood droplets across the counter's top. The cashier emitted a liquid cry of surprise and pain; he clutched his gushing throat in a futile attempt to quell the lifeblood that flowed from it and he stumbled backwards, hit the wall, then slid to the floor.

Peter (tuning out Seth's immediate whoops of pleasure) rounded the counter and planted his right boot in the cashier's left temple, knocking him to a prone position *and* unconscious in one fell swoop. The finishing touch had caught Peter's eye as soon as he had entered the store: a large sledgehammer. He didn't remember crossing the store and picking it up, but he hefted its weight in his hands and it felt *good.*

"Hey Petey, wasn't there a comedian that smashed fruit with a sledgehammer?" Seth.

"Yup." Peter said as he lifted the hammer high

over his head. "He died." He was reminded of an old metal song he heard when he was growing up:

See them try to bring the hammer down,
No damn chains can hold me to the ground.

He brought the hammer down, letting gravity do most of the work. Blood, brain tissue, and the cashier's last thoughts splattered all over Peter's boots in a wave of crimson warmth; Seth's midnight black Vans were spotless, of course, even though he stood right next to Peter. There were soft, puttering sounds as gobs of brain broke free from their surrounding membrane and leaked onto the floor; the smell of shit in the air was strong from the body's last expulsion before the cashier ceased to be among the living.

Seth put a pale, long-fingered hand on Peter's shoulder and gave it a squeeze. "Well done, Petey m'boy. A regular masterpiece."

"You think so?" Peter asked, dropping the hammer and looking at his victim through squared thumbs and forefingers, like an artist looking at a painting. He did, after all, consider himself to be an artist.

Seth smiled. "Absolutely."

Peter mimicked the smile. “Great.” He wiped down the handle of the hammer with a nearby rag, and snatched his bag of goodies off the blood-spattered counter. “Let’s jet. I got a date and I need new shoes.”

\- -

Take-Out

"Did you see that guy's *head?* It exploded like an obese man's heart at a deep-fried buffet!" Death always seemed to put Seth in a good mood.

"Of course I saw it. Hell, I *caused* it." Peter stated proudly, turning onto Jackson Street. "But it surely was somethin' else, wasn't it?" *Where the hell is that store?* "The hammer stood out to me from the beginning, you know. I knew it was the right choice."

"You're quite an artist, Petey." Seth leaned forward and pointed at a strip mall coming up on their left. "There it is."

"Thanks." Peter turned into the parking lot, not noticing that he hadn't asked about the store out loud or even mentioned what store he was looking for.

Obtaining new boots without any bloodshed, Peter was back on the road and listening to Seth's everlasting mouth within a matter of minutes. He reached under the seat while stopped at a red light and pulled out a purple purse, rifled through it, then removed a woman's billfold from the chaos within.

"I knew you to be a paranoid-delusional, a psychopath, even a sadistic serial-killer, but I *never* figured you to be a petty thief." Such an odd thing, hearing a tone of disapproval in Seth's voice.

"Seth, simple Seth. It's much easier to kill people in the sanctity of their own home, where the expectation of a violent death is usually farthest from their minds. And how better to find the home of said stranger?" He held up a California Driver's license. The name Jeanine Carmichael and the address 1758 East Jay Street were printed on it in DMV's standard lettering, right below the picture of a heavy-set blond woman.

"Geez." Seth said with a look of disgust. "I thought you said she was dead gorgeous."

"I did." Peter replied with a grin. "And in time, I will have only been half-lying."

1758 East Jay Street was a cheerful two-story townhouse, preceded by a pristine lawn that was fully decorated with all manner of plastic animals.

There were no discernible lights on in the house from what Peter could see, and the driveway lay empty.

"Looks like nobody's home, Petey. Now what?" Seth looked downcast.

"Of course she's not home." Peter said in a matter-of-fact tone, driving past the house as if it were not their intended destination. "She's waitressing at Jenny's Bar-and-Grill until ten, then she'll stop at the Express Coffee on Jacob avenue for a vanilla latte, Wong Fu's for her dry-cleaning, and she'll arrive here at around ten-forty." It was her nightly routine, the demise of so many victims of violent crimes.

"If you knew she wasn't going to be here, then what's the plan of action?"

"Well," Peter started, grabbing his bag of goodies from the floorboard. "First we have to park the car somewhere, then we have to break in."

The break-in was comically simple. There was a lattice-work structure built into the rear of the house to allow some sort of vine (as well as Peter himself) to climb it like a ladder, and an open window on the second floor sealed the deal.

Once inside, Seth whistled. In the master

bedroom (which was undoubtedly where they were) the grandeur nature of the furnishings and decorations suggested excessive wealth. A king-sized bed with an intricately carved frame and headboard took up only a small part of the room; there was also an enormous flat-screen on the wall surrounded by expensive (yet not original) artwork, a jacuzzi in the room's center, and a walk-in closet that contended with Peter's apartment in size (and probably worth, judging from the brand names on the clothing that overflowed from it's depths).

"*Look* at this shit." Said said incredulously. "She definitely must come from money, Petey boy, because there is no way in Hell she could afford shit like this on a waitress' salary. There are probably *celebrities* that couldn't afford all this shit." He scanned the room with greedy eyes. "Looks like we hit the jackpot."

"So it would seem."

"Now what?"

"We wait." *We wait for death's date, for she never seems to be late.*

At ten forty-six, a silver Lexus pulled up in the driveway and extinguished its lights. The overweight blond waitress got out of the car with some difficulty, then walked to the door, fumbling with her keys and dry-cleaning in hand.

Seth peered out the window and grimaced. "She looks like a shaved gorilla wearing a blond wig."

Peter had already taken up post in front of the bedroom door, listening for footsteps. When he heard them clunking down the hallway outside the door, he readied himself, mentally picturing his body as a coiled spring ready to explode into motion. As soon as he saw the doorknob start to turn, he drew back and kicked the door with all his might, disintegrating the latch mechanism; the door knocked the woman standing on the other side backward against the guard railing, while at the same time smashing countless thousands of dollars worth of rhinoplasty. Peter rushed forward as the blond started to moan in pain, clutching her gushing nose with both hands, and lifted her by the ankles up and over the railing. She plummeted at roughly the same speed a semi-truck would fall, hardly having time to yell out before striking the hardwood floor headfirst with a sickening *thwack!*

Seth leaned over the railing and peered at the broken body, still twitching as severed nerve endings fired for the last time, then looked back at Peter with an amused smile. "To be honest, I feel a little cheated."

Peter looked over the railing at his work, then back at Seth, grinning. "I'm not done yet, because she's not dead yet." They both descended the stairs and confirmed that the waitress lived indeed, and was only paralyzed. She was moaning softly; blood trickled from her nose, mouth, and ear canals.

"Okay." Seth said, crossing his arms over his narrow chest. "What's the grand finale?"

"Just watch." Peter said as he entered the kitchen, retrieving a serrated carving knife and a few turkey-sized freezer bags, while also spotting the second device involved in his evil scheme. He came back and used the knife to remove the waitress' pants. "Oh yeah." He said, remembering something. He flipped her over and slapped the fleshy part of her rump.

"There you go, Jeremy."

Seth rolled his eyes.

Peter then cut a steak-sized hunk of meat from each of the helpless woman's thighs, laying them neatly upon the small of her back, and zip-tied a freezer bag over her head. As she lay face-down, aspirating on the bloody foam that filled her oxygen-starved lungs, Peter took the chunks of meat over to the meat-grinder (the second object of the scheme), ground the meat, and bagged it in another freezer bag.

Seth observed all this with his strange, ever-bemused smile. “What *are* you doing? Are you really going to try your hand at cannibalism now?”

Peter squeezed the bag of leg-meat and smiled. “Now Seth, you can’t be afraid to try new things; this is 2008.” He laughed. “Besides, I won’t be the only one dining tonight.”

* * * *

“Hey Jeremy! I brought vittles!” Peter announced as he crossed the threshold of their grungy apartment, carrying a bag of greasy death.

Jeremy was still up, centered on the television. “Hey Pete.” Then immediately after, “Did you slap her ass, or what.” Jeremy, ever the clown.

“Yup. You hungry?”

“Yeah. What kind of grub ya got?”

“Veggie burgers.” It was all Peter could do to keep a straight face.

- -

No Room for Politics

Jeremy switched the TV to the Political Debate Show. "Oh, good lord. You *see* this bullshit? Can you believe the rejects that this country elects into office?" Politics was a subject that easily aggravated Jeremy. Sometimes Peter would listen to him rant for hours, about war, about corporate conspiracy, and on rare occasions, Manchurian candidates.

"It must be a tough job, having to make all those decisions. Having to deal with the stress and weight of all that responsibility." Peter commented thoughtfully.

Jeremy laughed. "Yeah, fucking-A right." He set the remote down and hunted through the ashtray for a sizable roach. "All that stress must've affected their judgment. Just look at the legalization of gay marriage. Only some crazies would approve that fudge-packing nonsense. Other screw-ups and indecisions I can name, just off the top of my head: the war in Iraq, the inability to kill Bin Laden, global warming, gas prices, the budget deficit, our debt to China, and the war on Marijuana." He took this opportune moment to pause and light his roach, puffing thoughtfully. "I mean, cannabis was legal back in the days before prohibition, but then they criminalize it, and legalize alcohol instead. That was a great I-fuckin-dea, alcohol kills six-and-a-half times more people then *all* the other drugs combined. So, in 1996, the great state of California passed Proposition 215, legalizing marijuana again for medical users, but federal task forces still continue to bust and incarcerate these people without contest. I think they're just pissed that they're losing out on all their black market money."

Peter just shook his head, amused by his friend's rant. "When you're right, you're right."

Jeremy raised his hands, palms-up, as if to say 'was there any doubt?'

Peter smiled, thinking: *madness has no room for politics.*

\- -

Justifiable Sins

At 8:56 PM, the Blakefield P.D. received report of a murder.

Under strict instructions from the chief of police, a special phone call had to be made before any homicide procedures could take place.

Lieutenant Sherridon tapped his fingers on the desk impatiently as the line rang for the fourth time. On the fifth ring a man answered. "Castor."

"Hello, this is Lieutenant Ryan Sherridon with the Blakefield Police Department. I was instructed to inform you that we received a report of a homicide at 1327 Arden Heights."

"Thank you, Lieutenant." There was a soft click as the line went dead.

Detective John Castor hung up the phone. "Reuben. We got one." He powered down the laptop he had been working on and stood from his desk.

His partner, Reuben Pollux, mimicked these

movements, and they proceeded through the outer corridor to the parking garage.

Immediately upon their arrival at 1327 Arden Heights (Dillon's Hardware Emporium), Detectives Castor and Pollux were greeted by the Blakefield P.D., and after a brief flash of their badges, were shown to the crime scene.

"What happened here?" Pollux asked the on-scene pathologist.

"Well sir, the murder weapon was obviously that bloody sledgehammer over there, but judging from the blood-splatter pattern on the counter and the wound itself, the killer first incapacitated the victim by slicing him here," He indicated a wound on the victim's neck, one that paled in comparison to the bloody mess that lay mere inches above. "And he must've used a very sharp blade, because there is little tearing of epidermal and arterial tissues."

"What about a utility knife?" Castor's question came from behind them. "There's a receipt in the register for the purchase of a Craftsman utility knife. The receipt still being in the register would lead one to believe that it was the last purchase before the murder, possibly belonging to the killer himself."

The pathologist nodded. “That’s a reasonably sound conclusion.”

“Okay, so the killer made the purchase, used the utility knife to slit the man’s throat, then crushed his skull with a...what, ten-pound sledgehammer?” Pollux asked.

“Twelve. But yes, that would be my professional analysis, based on the facts-at-hand.” The pathologist replied, then his face displayed a worried look. “But I can’t reason a motive into the equation. There was no money or merchandise taken from what we can tell, aside from purchased items, and that in itself is odd, *the killer paid for his stuff.”* He shook his head. “Why kill the cashier?”

“Reuben, look at this.” Castor interrupted. He had put on rubber gloves and was examining the receipt.

“What?”

“Look at these items.” He handed Pollux the receipt. “A knife, drill, zip ties...” He trailed off.

Pollux studied the items and caught what his partner was driving at. “This wasn’t a one-time thing. The killer plans to do it again.”

“What?” The pathologist asked, overhearing the two detectives’ conversation. “You think that we have a serial killer?”

"Yes, it's seems that may be the case." Pollux motioned to Castor. "Come on, John." Then to the pathologist, he said, "Find out if there was any surveillance videos, either from the store or surrounding areas, that may have caught a glimpse of our sicko or his vehicle. You and your department can take care of things from here; give me daily progress reports on anything that comes up."

"Ten-four."

Once back in the car, Pollux speed-dialed a number on his cell. It rang twice before being answered by a female voice. "Authorization, please."

"Pollux, operative number six-one-three-eight." There was a slight pause as voice recognition software analyzed his speech patterns, then a soft click as he was transferred to his handler.

"Report." The handler's voice was encrypted, giving it an odd, kidnapper-demanding-a-ransom quality.

"We have reason to believe that there is a thrill-killer on the loose in Blakefield."

"How many dead?"

"Only one discovered, evidence shows preparation for a second. The gruesome nature of the crime hints of severe mental instability." Pollux stated. "What are our orders, sir?"

There was a pause. "Assist the Blakefield P.D. with their investigation, and when a break in the case uncovers the perpetrator, eliminate the suspect. Complete your task by any means necessary, but try to do it discreetly, our employer doesn't want any collateral damage."

"Yes, sir." Pollux hung up the phone and relayed the message to Castor.

"Let's get to it, brother."

- -

Song of Death

Peter's childhood, if that's what you called it, was spent without the kindness and care that most parents exhibit towards their children; his mother died while giving birth to him, and the loss drove his father to insanity.

Peter could not get along with the kids at his school because of his loner attitude. He segregated himself from other children, and was made fun of for it; he was teased daily and sometimes beaten badly by older kids. He would come home with dirty clothes, black-eyes, and bruises, then his father would punish him for fighting.

When he was eleven, after receiving a serious beating from his father for a fight that he had neither started nor wanted to participate in, Peter decided that he'd had enough, and ran away.

He survived by stealing food from various stores and houses, and slept under the Wayport bridge at night, listening to the peaceful sound of the river as it made its way to join with the Pacific ocean. It was under this bridge that he first encountered the man named Seth.

Peter sat on a rock, eating a meal of crackers and potted meat, when his concentration was broken by the sound of a greeting voice. He looked up to find a thin, smiling man watching him with bright, youthful eyes. He had black hair, and was dressed in similarly-colored attire: black hooded-sweatshirt, black jeans, and black boots. Though he was a creepy-looking fellow, Peter wasn't afraid of him in the least; the only person he was ever afraid of was Amos.

"Hello." The creepy man greeted for the second time, still smiling. "Excuse me, but would you mind very much if I rested here under your bridge for a while? I've traveled a long ways, and I need to rest my weary bones."

Peter shrugged. "Yeah, that's fine with me." He held up his crackers and the potted meat. "You hungry, mister?"

The man shook his head and sat down cross-legged a short distance away from Peter. "No thanks friend. And the name's Seth." Still smiling, as if the world was a joke that only he understood.

"I'm Peter."

"Pleasure to meet you, Peter." Then he asked, "Do you like to read very much?"

"No. Not really."

"Oh. 'I see' said the blind man to his deaf son."

Peter liked talking with Seth. He seemed to have just as many animosities for the world as Peter did, and sometimes their conversations would remind him of those few, lucid moments when his father would talk with him like a normal person; they would laugh, tell each other stories, and have a wonderful time.

But sometimes Seth would talk about something he called 'the veil,' and about things like the infinities of space, time, and death. These topics made Peter uneasy, but the feeling of uneasiness was negated by the feeling of companionship; he was just happy to not be alone.

Three-and-a-half months after his escape from the madhouse that he called home, the police caught up with Peter. An officer performing a random check for vandalism and drug offenders spotted Peter's camp under the bridge one day, while Seth was out looking for work. When first questioned, Peter would not tell the officer his name, but when he was threatened with being taken to jail, he explained everything that led to his current situation. The officer listened intently, with that practiced look of sympathetic understanding that every police officer emits, until Peter had said his fill, then told Peter that everything was going to be okay, just get into the cruiser. Peter did as the officer instructed. To Peter's dismay, the officer took him straight home, pulling into the driveway with cruiser lights flashing red-and-blue.

Peter's father, Amos, emerged from the house warily, like a rattlesnake emerging from its den.

The officer exited the cruiser and let Peter out of the backseat. "I found your boy camping down under the Wayport bridge, Amos, looks like he was there for a while."

"Oh God, thank you so much. I was so worried about him." Amos said, feigning concern. "Ever since my wife died, he's been all I got. I don't know what I'd do without him." Peter was unaware that any person as far beyond insanity as his father could ever act so well.

"Well, he's safe now." The well-intentioned gesture, which would very likely cause the infliction of pain and violence, was done, and Peter saw no escape. "Go on now, son." The officer gave Peter a gentle push in the direction of his father. "Reap the consequences." Consenting defeat, Peter reluctantly approached Amos.

Amos grabbed him in a fierce hug that may have looked, to the to the untrained eye, like one delivered by a parent that was happy to see their child home safe; in actuality, it was a painful warning that nearly broke his back, and clearly stated: *you're gonna get it.*

"Okay now, you folks take care." The officer said pleasantly, no doubt feeling quite good about himself, then got in his cruiser and sped off.

Amos looked down at Peter with maddened eyes. "I thought the devil had come and taken you earlier than expected, until you showed up with that piggy. Maybe I'll just send you myself, all nice and gift-wrapped like a trussed Sunday-goose." He grabbed Peter by the arm, *hard*, and dragged him into the depths of the house, to the large underground storage that had originally been intended to serve as a wine cellar. Amos opened the door and threw him down the wooden flight of stairs. "Here you'll stay, you little demon. You'll stay until the devil comes for you, either through me or personally." Amos locked the door with a click that resounded throughout the cellar that was devoid of light.

Amos kept him in the dungeon for six days and six nights without food or water. In his delirium, Peter was visited by Seth (only this was not the Seth that he had met under the bridge, this was some other, sinister Seth, who told him that everything was going to be okay. And terrible things, as well. *This* Seth gave him a tack-hammer, calling it his "little gift of hope."

On the morning of the seventh day, Amos came through the door and stood at the top of the dark stairs, staring down into the blackness where Peter (a new Peter) lurked like a hungry animal that had spotted its prey. The kitchen knife in Amos' hand glinted as he flicked on the light switch, then slowly started to descend the stairs.

Peter stood with his back to the wall, the hammer concealed behind him, and Seth's voice echoed in his mind. *Your little gift of hope.*

"Let's play, Petey." Amos said with an anticipated finality, raising the knife.

PING! The tack-hammer smashed into Amos' temple with a dull musical note, causing him to reel backwards and drop the knife to the floor with a clatter. *PING!* Peter landed a second vicious blow to Amos' left kneecap, exploding it in its socket and dropping him to the floor. *PING! PING! PING! PING!* The hammer sang a song of death as Peter unleashed a flurry of solid blows to Amos' skull, turning it into a bloody mass of broken bone and brain-tissue. Though his face and shirt were soaked in his father's blood, Peter continued to swing until his arm was heavy and his muscles burned.

Long after Amos was dead, when he was completely satisfied, Peter ceased his murderous assault, then climbed the stairs and locked the door behind him. He went into the kitchen and made himself a much anticipated lunch: grilled cheese, chicken soup, and a glass of milk. When he was through, he poured a bottle of vegetable oil into the frying pan, overflowing it onto the stove, and then turned the burner on high.

Peter watched his childhood home burn to the ground from Sentry hill, with his new ethereal companion at his side. Now that he had the sea, he felt unstoppable; now that he had Seth, he no longer feared his own madness.

- -

Playtime (For Big Kids)

Peter (no longer the timid Petey of his past) sat on a stone bench in Brandiscomb park, watching the normal kids play their silly childhood games of tag, hide-and-seek, and red rover; he sat listening to Seth, the Whooptollie who was the embodiment of his own psychological break. The day was overcast and smelled of acrid smoke, and the distant bleating of sirens could be heard over the sounds of children at play in their own little worlds.

We all have our own little worlds, Petey. Seth was a constant voice in his head, and though Peter did not understand everything that he said (much like he didn't understand his father), he listened intently. *They're all connected like spiderwebs, like wheels on a spoke. And the Sea is their center; the center of all the multi-verse. They play, and their imagination takes them to another world; what is little known, though, is that those places are* real. *Everything is real.*

In the park, Peter noticed a group of older children harassing a young, slightly overweight boy that was wearing a coat which looked like it may have been bought from a thrift store; the four older boys took turns pushing him back and forth between them, laughing and calling him something that Peter couldn't quite make out (but no doubt it had something to do with the boy's weight). There was one thing that Peter *could* make out, though: the boy was crying.

The biggest of the group then punched the boy in the stomach, bringing him to his knees; the other boys followed suit, clouting the poor boy with haphazard blows. The group's victim pleaded for mercy through cries of pain, trying desperately to shield himself from the fusillade of fists.

Before Peter even knew what he was doing, he was on his feet and marching towards the fray. Upon further reflection, he realized how much the act of bullying affected him. He was *furious;* furious that they had the audacity to pick on someone as docile-looking as the boy in question, and he planned to *do* something about it.

"What are you doing?" Peter asked as he neared the group, but no one paid him any attention. "Hey! Quit it!" Hey! YOU GODDAMN SONS'A'BITCHES

QUIT!!!" Peter roared (and was reminded of his father while doing so), finally losing the last bit of his patience; patience that was already fast becoming an endangered species.

The attackers ceased their assault all at once, looking at Peter with shocked expressions; the beaten boy tried to get away, but was held in place (almost as an afterthought) by a boy that Amos most certainly would have described as a *'corn fed little sum-bitch.'*

The assumed leader of the group stepped forward. "What'chu want young'n? You wanna' beatin' s'well?" The boy couldn't have been much older than fifteen (from the sound of it, probably not an honor student either) and was built like a truck; he wore a baseball cap that stated: *I'm a Country boy!*

His followers snickered, apparently impressed with Country boy's macho attitude.

"Actually," Peter began. "I want you and your friends to leave him the *fuck* alone."

The followers fell silent, looking to their leader for a reaction. Country boy looked startled for a moment, then let out a laugh that made his voice crack when he next spoke. "You shittin' me, youngster? You better git outta here 'fore you get hurt."

It was Peter's turn to smile. "If you don't leave that kid alone, I'll show you what it's like to *really* hurt."

The followers gaped with open-mouthed expressions of shock; Country boy's amused look fell away to anger, which, impossible as it seemed, made it even harder to understand his thick southern drawl. "Im'a have'ta teach you a less'n 'en." He muttered while confidently striding forward, then grabbed Peter by the neck with his right hand.

Peter's own right hand struck out with web-and forefinger, catching the bully's larynx and driving him backward in a choking fit. Immediately upon the release of Country boy's hand, Peter cocked back and swung as hard as he could, landing a blow about two inches below the would-be attacker's bellybutton, dropping him to his knees; if the blow had been delivered by someone a bit more powerful, it would have drove internal organs up against the spine, delivering a death blow, but the most damage Peter might have caused with his blow would be a little blood in the urine.

Peter took in the horrified look on the followers' faces with savage delight (as well as the grateful look from the group's first victim, who had slipped away to watch from a safe distance and tend his wounds) as they watched a younger, smaller boy beat their fearless leader's country ass with surprisingly little effort.

"*This* is what will happen to you if you mess with me or my friend again." He told them, then once again turned his attention to Country boy, who had sunk into the fetal position and was hacking (little flecks of blood could now be seen on his lips), holding his stomach. Peter knelt down and grabbed Country boy's right hand, then jerked the index finger in a 90-degree angle, emitting a loud *snap!* He demonstrated a similar process with the thumb of the right hand, and Country boy choked on a host of resulting screams of pain; a dark stain materialized in the crotch of his pants as he pissed himself.

People started to notice the scene, and the followers quickly dispersed (bringing to mind the frenzied escape of cockroaches when the light is flipped on); soon the cops would arrive. Peter decided not to exact his full revenge (lucky for Country boy, for he would surely have died) and instead made his way to where the original victim was standing. "Hey, are you okay?"

The boy (whose nose and mouth both still

displayed traces of drying blood) nodded excitedly. "Oh yes! Thank you so much! I can't believe you whipped Trevor Anderson in front of *all his friends!*"

Peter laughed (for the first time in several years). "Who, old Country boy?" He shrugged. "You know what they say, 'the bigger they are, the harder they fall.'"

The boy waited, and when it was apparent that Peter was not going to explain, he asked, "What *who* says?"

Oh lord. Peter thought to himself. *I rescued the village idiot.* "Uh, never mind. I'm Peter." He extended his hand.

"Jeremy." The boy said, and grabbed Peter's hand, giving it a vigorous shake. "Jeremy Watters." That look of heartfelt gratitude was still there, and it softened Peter's petrified heart (if only just a little).

"Well, Jeremy Watters, why don't we make like zeh' tree." Then, remembering who he was talking to, added, "And leave."

Jeremy nodded. "Alright." Then a look of embarrassment came across his face. "Hey, uh, I'd understand if you didn't want to, but...my mom is probably almost finished with dinner, and uh, well..." He hesitated, unsure of how to finish; not wanting to say 'I'm afraid to walk home.'

Peter made it easy on him. “Yeah, I’ll come with you.” He smiled. “I can help explain what happened.”

“Okay, and we’ll have vittles, too.”

“Sounds great, I’m famished.” Peter replied, genuinely surprised that a person like Jeremy even *knew* a word like ‘vittles.’ Upon receiving a blank look, he amended by saying, “I mean, I’m hella’ hungry.”

Peter found that the widow Maybel Watters, Jeremy’s mother, was the nicest person that he had ever encountered, and perhaps the most protective as well.

“Oh-my-goodness-sweety-what-happened!!?” Maybel cried out when she saw the two boys walk through the door, and ran to her son’s side.

“Mom, it’s okay.” Jeremy said, trying to hold back his mother’s frenzied attempts to sop his bloodied face with her dishrag. “I just got jumped, that’s all.”

Maybel’s face displayed a looked of puzzled concern. “You jumped into *what*?”

Peter took this pause as an opportunity to ‘jump’ in. “He was attacked by a group of older boys, Mrs. Watters.”

Maybel turned her attention to the stranger that

she was only moments ago completely unaware of, and seemed slightly embarrassed at her outburst of motherly concern. “Oh my, I didn’t see you there. Are you a friend of Jeremy’s?”

Peter glanced at Jeremy for a second, then said, “Yeah. We just met today.”

With that curiosity quelled and the info safely stowed away in the recesses of her mind, Maybel once again turned to Jeremy. “So you were attacked?”

Jeremy nodded and lowered his head, ashamed. “Yeah.” Then he perked up a little. “But Peter made them stop. He-“

Oh shit, don’t tell her about the fingers. Please don’t tell her about the fingers.

“- told them they’d better stop hurting me, *or else…*” He finished, adding a comically sinister tone to his voice on the last part.

For a moment, Peter thought that Maybel was going to ask more questions about how he had managed to stop a crowd of violent boys by himself, and that he’d be forced to concoct some lie on the spot, but she didn’t.

“Thank you for protecting Jeremy.” She said, tears welling up in her eyes, which she set to wiping with her apron. “It’s just been so hard for us since my husband died."

Peter suddenly wondered what it would be like to have a mother, or anyone for that matter, that cared about him. "It's hard to lose someone you love." He was silent for a moment before speaking again. "My mother died when I was born, and I just recently lost my father."

Oh you poor dear!" Maybel said. "Do you have any other family?"

Peter shook his head.

"What will become of you?"

Peter shrugged. "I think the next step is a group home. Then, *if* I'm really lucky, maybe foster parents. The odds of a couple wanting a child my age are slim, though."

Maybel was quiet for a long time, apparently trying to decide something she considered very important. When she spoke, it made Peter's heart crack with gratitude (perhaps the first real gratitude that he had ever really known). "Peter...I know we've only just met, but...I want you to know that you can stay here with us. If you want, that is." Her sincere compassion was almost too much for Peter to bear.

"Ma'am, I would be honored."

Over the following years he and Jeremy went through school (he under an assumed last name to avoid the police) Peter wondered about Maybel Watters' decision to simply let him stay (with absolutely no evidence of truth in the story of his parents' demise, and with no legal documentation whatsoever), then came to a realization: sometimes people's needs overcome their sense of reality, and they willingly believe anything.

- -

Doorways

Peter drove his Camaro down 3rd Street in silence. For once, Seth's everlasting mouth was not droning on about endless violence, the eternity within the trail of a tear, or some equally disturbing subject; he only stared thoughtfully out the window at the passing suburbanite homes. It was possible, judging from his distant look, that he was puzzling over some great physics problem involving a great depth of concentration, or even contemplating the purpose of life itself, but Peter knew better. Peter had found himself in a similar positions many times over the years, staring distantly, yet utterly absorbed in that distance; peering into that world of everlasting twilight, where the Whooptollies first came to him with their dark ideas and hate, whispering softly into his ear like so many insects. Yes, even with infinite other possibilities, Peter was certain that Seth was staring at that pool of lunacy that they both knew so well. Amos' maddened sea.

Peter turned onto Canaan Avenue, trying to conceive new inventive ways to kill; two blocks of asphalt later, a pale hand touched his shoulder.

"Stop here, Petey."

Peter did as he was asked. "What is it, Seth?"

"There is an event coming." Before Peter had time to ask another question, Seth pointed to a spot that was further down the road.

An event? Peter looked were Seth was pointing and did not see anything at first, but then noticed what his companion must have been gesturing to; what he saw did not impress him in the least.

"It's a dog." He stated flatly.

On the sidewalk about two and a half blocks down the road from where the Camaro idled, sat a large German Shepherd. It regarded them with intent eyes, and its silent gaze unnerved Peter for some reason that he could not explain.

Seth leaned forward with a smug grin proudly displayed on his pale face. "Is that your final answer?"

His companion's cryptic question did not trouble him half as much as the canine itself, but it certainly did little to ease Peter's sudden wariness. "I *hate* it when you do that." He said, irritated. "Why can't you ever just tell me what's going on?"

Seth just smiled his little smile; that damned *everlasting* smile. "Because you already know."

"I know what?"

"Just look, Petey. Here he comes."

The dog had gotten up while Peter wasn't looking and was walking toward them. Then it suddenly broke into a full sprint; charging toward them like a maddened hell-hound in sight of its quarry. Flecks of foam flew from its mouth with each laborious breath as it closed the two block distance with alarming speed; Peter could feel madness emanating from the beast in feverish waves.

In the last feet of the dog's insane sprint it leaped into the air, teeth bared, and smacked head-on into the Camaro's front-side passenger fender with every ounce of mustered momentum that a two block sprint could create; the only resulting sounds were the skull's impact upon metal, the bone collapsing in on itself, and Seth's immediate burst of gleeful laughter. The dog did not utter a single growl, bark, or yelp preceding or following its apparent suicide.

Peter turned to Seth with a perplexed look on his face. "What the hell was *that*?"

Seth laid an index finger under his nose,

pantomiming the '*shh*' gesture, then pointed back out the window.

Peter turned in time to see a shadowy silhouette emerge from the canine corpse, like smoke escaping from a fresh bullet-hole, and materialize into the shape of man; a man who surely could have been Seth's twin.

The doppleganger mirrored one of Seth's bemused, all-knowing grins, sending a chill down Peter's spine, and then *shimmered* out of existence; not an immediate ceasing of existence, as if nothing had been there in the first place, but a delayed, mirage-like disappearance. For some reason that shimmering

(Shearing, it's called Shearing)

reminded Peter of Amos' cellar. Something that had happened in that cellar, following Amos' death.

(Now you've got it)

"No." Peter said aloud, struggling within himself. "I don't like doing this. I don't like *remembering.*"

But it was not as if he had a choice, was it?

The fifth day in the cellar was devoid of all light and smelled of urine, because after three, Petey had not been able to hold it any longer. The blackness threatened to consume his soul with despair because it was so dark, so dark*, and he just wanted to* die. *If Amos had chosen that particular moment to descend the stairs with that gleaming knife and gut his son like a fish, Petey would have welcomed it; he probably would have smiled while the deed was done and even thanked him subsequently as he lay bleeding. But it was cold and lonely and dank in that cellar, and there was a whispering; a soft shirring noise that was the argument against insanity slowly falling away into the depths of the icy darkness.*

Petey focused on that noise through closed eyes, the sound of sanity and insanity sliding on one another, the shuffling sound of the parallel, and the stress of it caused the fabric of the veil to part. (Shear) He opened his eyes and saw a hairline thread, floating in front of his vision like a blind spot acquired from staring at the sun too long.

He reached out his hand and touched that crack in the world's lining; a crack that was really a tear, a tear that was really a doorway. Petey stepped through that doorway and glimpsed another world. Another reality. Another level in the tower of madness.

(Can you say all aboard?)

Peter snapped back into focus; into the present

reality of *now.* "What was the point of remembering *that*?" He asked angrily. "That shit wasn't real. I was delusional from lack of food and water."

"Oh but it *was* real, Petey." Seth assured him. "Don't you get it? *Everything* is real. I told you that once before."

"Why is it so important, then?"

Seth sat back in his seat, turning to gaze out the window at the neighbors who were gathering on the sidewalk, drawn like flies to the smell of death. "Not *everyone* can do that, you know. Not everyone can S*hear* their way into another world, Petey. You never know, it might come in handy sometime."

Peter shook his head. "Even if I *could* do it again, I don't think I could make myself go back there."

"Come now, Petey. My world isn't so bad, is it?"

Peter left that one unanswered. The truth was that Seth's world was *beautiful.* The only problem was that when you went *there,* it was ever so easy to get distracted; when you were *there* the tear stayed open, allowing what was on the other side to *slip* through. Like Seth. But not all of Seth's kin were as nice as he was, were they?

Petey stood there, holding the hammer that dripped with Amos' blood in the dank cellar, and nearly fainted. He watched as black, sooty smoke rose from the gaping wound in Amos' head in searching tendrils, and came together in the form of a grinning apparition, much the same as it had through the tear that he first created, and much the same as it would many years later, from the corpse of a German Shepherd.

'Amos was not a madman,' Petey realized, once again sitting in his Camaro. 'He was possessed by another Seth; a Whooptolly from the world of the maddening sea. As I am possessed by one now.'

"Is that how you think of our relationship, Petey?" Seth asked with a tone of irritation that Peter had never heard before. "Possession? Control? Shit Petey, I've *never* controlled you like my brethren did your father."

"I bet you tried, though." Peter knew this was true; it was *how* he knew it was true that was the eluded truth. He knew that he and his father were different somehow, and that the difference kept him from being manipulated, while Amos was consumed. It also gave Peter *control;* it gave him an idea of how to become well again.

Seth grasped his host's thought through the link

that they shared, and it made him angry. "You're a smart kid, Petey. But you don't want to tempt the devil." He bared his teeth; this time, he wasn't smiling. "*You don't want to fuck with me.* I may not be able to do much to *you* more than influence your thoughts, but as long as you live, I *can* affect the world. You've seen me kill."

Peter weighed his next words carefully. "What are you trying to say, Seth?"

Seth's smile returned. "Peter, simple, Peter." Seth dropped the playful 'Petey,' another first. "I'm not *trying* to say anything. I'm *telling* you that if you do something stupid, I'm going to eliminate the only thing in this world that you even remotely care about."

Oh no. Jeremy.

"Oh yes, Petey. Better believe that."

- -

Into the Frying Pan

The fax containing the news came in while Castor and Pollux were finishing up paperwork on a previous case. Blakefield Police had another murder, this one even more horrendous than the previous; the underlined phrase 'suspected cannibalism,' definitely conceded to that point.

Upon arrival, the two detectives were shown to the crime scene. It wasn't quite as messy as the hardware store murder, but it had it's own twisted flavor; many of the on-scene investigators sported thick gobs of menthol under their noses to mask the nauseating odor of cooked human flesh in the air.

"What do you have for us, Pat?" Pollux asked Blakefield's leading on-scene pathologist.

"The main cause of death was asphyxiation." He gestured to the bag zip-tied over the woman's head. "Also, there are two large sections of flesh missing from the thigh areas of both legs which, I assume from the horrid stench in the air, the suspect cooked on the range and quite possibly *ate.*" He shuddered. "And also the victim's neck appears to be broken."

Pollux glanced at the dead woman's neck, which was cocked at a gruesome angle. *Gee, you think?* "So you say the suspect…cooked?"

"That's right."

"Did you dust for prints? He must have touched something."

"No sir. We have strict orders to wait until you conduct *your* investigation. My theory is based entirely on speculation at this point."

Castor decided to join the conversation. "I think it was the same guy, Reuben."

"How's that?"

Castor used a ballpoint pen to point at the small piece of plastic that fastened the plastic bag. "The zip tie is the same size and brand as the ones bought at the hardware store."

Pollux studied the object that was in question. "You're right, John."

Further investigation of the crime scene revealed countless sets of prints, but most belonged to the victim herself, and still others belonged to various staff members that she employed. There was one set that *was* of interest to the investigators, though; a full right hand set of fingerprints on the handle of the meat grinder.

Blakefield P.D.'s own database yielded no results; often local murders go unsolved due to mere lack of resources. When Castor cross-referenced the fingerprints in the ASK (Active Serial-Killer) database he got a sixteen point match from data files documenting the "Guardian Angel" project.

The G.A. Project, a Lucette County Ordinance that was passed (then later shut down, due to misused grants) in order to provide extra safety for children, stated that all children that were born after the year 1985 had to fingerprinted, then logged into a central database. Funny that even after discontinuation, the project still yielded results.

Peter Ardula. Last known residence; Wayport Valley, California.

"Gotcha', you bastard."

The list of people in Ardula's age bracket that resided in Wayport Valley (hoping that he still lived there was a long shot) was short, and of course there was no hit with the suspects actual name;

Castor assumed that there was an alias involved.

Castor and Pollux visited the homes of each of the fourteen names on the list, questioning the residents about whether or not they knew the suspect. All of the people questioned denied ever having known the man, but one person seemed to the detectives like he wasn't telling the truth, and they decided to put him on the top of their 'persons of interest' list.

His name was Jeremy Watters.

\- -

Desperate Measures

Peter returned to his apartment absolutely disgusted with himself. Seth had used his leverage to get him to strangle a beautiful Swedish tennis instructor whom he had begun to develop an attraction to; to make matters worse, Seth didn't even let him follow the woman to a secluded area, instead making him do the deed in a seedy public restroom where he could have been caught at any time. It was stupid and unplanned and just so...*Seth.*

Jeremy looked very pale as he sat on the couch, wringing his hands together nervously, and his mouth opened like a floodgate at the sight of his roommate. "Jesus Peter, where the hell you *been*? You got *cops* looking for you, man." He held out an engraved business card, and Peter took it with a sinking feeling. "These two cats in Columbine suits showed up about an hour or two ago, asking about you. I played dumb and told them that I didn't know anyone named Peter Are-do-whatever-the-fuck." He gave Peter a worried look. "Dude, you know I *hate* cops. What did you *do*?"

The feeling of dreadful panic gnawed at the lining of his stomach, but Peter managed a laugh that was credible enough.

"*Jeremy.* Calm down."

"Why the hell should I *calm down?!* The damn cops show up at the door with all their questions while I got weed in the house and you want me to *calm-*"

"My last name is Dobbs. Peter Henry Dobbs. Not whatever you said."

Jeremy stopped shouting. "What?"

"My. Name. Is. Dobbs."

"You mean, they're not looking for you?"

Peter shook his head. "No. Not me."

Jeremy exhaled a sigh of relief. "Oh, good. No worries, then." He reached under the couch, fumbled for a second, then pulled out his pot-tin. "Good thing I wasn't blazed when they came."

Peter looked at the card. The only thing on it was a phone number with an out-of-state area code; there was no department name or identifying features, just a number.

Interesting.

Peter had a plan; he went into his sparsely decorated room, reached under the bed, and pulled out a small fireproof lock-box. He opened it with a tiny key from his keyring, and extracted an immaculate 9mm Beretta, also removing two loaded clips and a 50 round box of ammo. He slid one of the clips into place with a sharp *click,* the other in his right pocket, then tucked the pistol into the back of his jeans, covering it with his shirt.

After grabbing his car keys and his coat (depositing the box of shells in one of the large, zip-up pockets), Peter told his roommate that he was going out.

"Going out? You just got here a few minutes ago."

"Yeah, I know. I'm just having a little trouble at work; it's got me a little wigged out." It wasn't necessarily that far from the truth.

Jeremy nodded sympathetically. "Yeah, I know what that's like." He held out his glass bing (which was in actuality a small bong, but he said it was too small to be considered a bong, that it looked like it was more of a bing). "Wanna rip? It'll help."

It was an old joke between the two; Jeremy knew that Peter didn't smoke, but he offered it nonetheless. Peter, to humor his ever easily-amused friend, always declined the same way. "Tempting, but no thanks."

Jeremy laughed. "*Fucker.* One of these days I'm gonna get you to smoke with me, you just wait and see. No one can withstand the Maryjane forever."

Peter, despite all he was going through, managed to smile; it was good to have a friend. "Maybe one day, but definitely not right now."

Peter left his apartment building thinking about the task before him, crossed the parking area, and got in his Camaro. After an uncomfortable moment of shifting in his seat, he decided to put the Beretta in the glove compartment.

"Where we going, Petey?" Seth asked from the backseat.

Peter didn't even bother to look back. "You know what I'm doing, Seth. Why do you ask if you already know?"

Seth smiled. "It amuses me. Because even though *you* know that I know, you still lie to me on occasion."

Peter drove into the neighboring town of Blakefield, searching for a good house; it was totally against his style to do anything like what he was about to do in broad daylight, but desperate times called for desperate measures, as the saying said. He had to protect Jeremy.

And the other thing, but that's not important because I can't think about it. It's important but if I think about it he'll notice, so it can't be important.

Peter spotted a black Mercedes as it pulled into the driveway of an expensive looking house with an immaculate lawn and a three-car garage. The driver parked in front of the expansive garage; an elderly man exited the vehicle, making his way to the front door with all the slow carefulness that one acquires with many years of age tucked under their belt.

Perfect.

Seth was upset. "*Fuck* that, Petey! That old fucker will probably die tomorrow on his own, let's find someone else."

"We don't have time." Peter drove a few streets down to a nearby park, and pulled next to the curb. He opened the glove compartment and retrieved the pistol inside, once again slipping it into the waistband of his jeans and hiding it with his shirt.

"Here goes." Peter said to himself (and Seth) as he got out of the car, and started walking toward the house of an old man whose life had just gotten a lot shorter.

As he climbed the steps to the front door, Peter

looked around to make sure that no one was looking, then confidently opened the door and strode in as if he owned the place. People seldom lock their doors in the daytime, when they first return home from wherever it is that they have arrived from; it's their time to relax.

Peter found the owner of the home doing just that, kicked back in a puffy leather chair with feet propped on a matching leather footrest.

At the sight of the gun, the old man raised his hands warily. "Oh, my God."

Peter shook his head. "Not even close. Get up."

* * * *

The phone rang.

As was customary, Castor let it ring five times before answering. "Castor."

The line was silent, save for someone's heavy breathing.

"Hello?"

"Hey there, piggy." A man's voice; elderly. "How's the crime catching business?"Castor sat up straight. "Who is this?"

There was a pause. Then, "I'm the one you've been searching for...in all the wrong places."

Castor waved his arm at Pollux and mouthed 'it's him.' Pollux nodded and began furiously tapping the keys on his laptop, initiating a trace on the phone call. "Is that so? Have you called to say that you've given up and want to turn yourself in?"

Another pause. "In a way. I called to let you know that you're off base."

Castor smiled. *Oh yeah?* "I don't think so, we have evidence. We found DNA at one of the crime scenes; we know who you are Mr. Ardula, and it's only a matter of time before we track you down."

A longer pause. "I don't know what you think you've found...but you got the wrong guy."

"We have your fingerprints on an object used to mutilate one of the victims."

Pause. "I wear surgical latex when I work...you don't have *my* fingerprints, Friday."

Castor's smile evaporated. "If you're not Ardula, and not connected to his friend whose name I won't mention, how did you get this number?"

Pause. "I have my ways, Friday...why don't you ask the Chief of Police? I have to go now...there is more work to be done...I'll be in touch." The line went dead.

Castor turned to his partner. "Did you get the trace?"

Pollux nodded. “327 Jenova Street, Blakefield.”

“Good, let’s go. We’ll either catch him before he leaves, or we’ll wait and get him when he comes back.”

“If he comes back.” Pollux noted.

* * * *

The elderly man hung up the phone. “Now what? I’ve said everything that you wanted me to say.”

Peter regarded the senior with stone eyes. “Do you have any guns?”

The man nodded. “Yes. I have a pistol in the top drawer of my dresser, and a shotgun in my bedroom closet.”

“Perfect.”

- -

Into the Belly of the Beast

Castor and Pollux arrived at 327 Jenova Street in record time, though they broke nearly every traffic law known to man along the way. They did not call in for backup, for they had their own agenda that the Blakefield Police just wouldn't understand. Regular law enforcement (hell, the world) wasn't ready for the unveiling of ASKET. Yet.

The two men got out of the car a few houses down the street and walked to the trunk, which Castor opened with the ignition key, revealing an arsenal that was fit for the city S.W.A.T. team.

"This is going to get messy." Pollux said, strapping on a bullet-proof vest.

"Don't I know it, brother."

"John, if something happens..." Pollux was silent for a moment, and the painful look in his eyes seemed strange as he stood there, donned in Kevlar and holding a fully-loaded Spaz-12 assault shotgun. "I just want you to know that I don't blame you for what you did."

Castor recoiled. His brother, Reuben, was referring to the death of their parents, as well as the hand that John had played in it.

Reuben nodded toward the house that contained the cannibalistic madman. "Let's get this bastard."

* * * *

The plan was simple. No, scratch that. The plan was just plain fucking *insane*; inspired by too many cheesy action movies and a whole lotta' *crazy*. The owner of the house was dead, lying on the floor only a few feet in front of the room's entrance. A single bullet to the brain from the old man's Smith and Wesson had taken care of that; *that* was simple. The only thing left was to wait, with the revolver in his gloved hand, for the front door to open.

Peter's intuition told him that the two 'detectives' would not call for backup; nor would they both enter from the same door. That was okay. Peter had the front door covered, it was the *back* door that posed a problem; a problem that was solved by the old man's double-barreled shotgun, a few zip-ties, and some fishing line. The resulting booby trap wasn't infallible, but it would sure put someone in a bad mood if they tripped the line just right.

MacGyver, eat your heart out.

* * * *

Castor stood outside the front door, dripping sweat in the heat of the summer day from the heaviness of the Kevlar. The plan was to wait 20 seconds, long enough for Pollux to make his way around to the back door, before hammering his way through the obstruction and shooting at anything that wasn't his brother.

He looked at his wristwatch, watching the second hand as closely as a junkie watching the dealer weigh out his fix.

5, 4, 3, 2, 1…

Castor kicked the front door open (the frame splitting with a boom that seemed too loud; almost like a shotgun) and was greeted by the body of an old man, lying face down in a pool of congealed blood, just a few feet in front of him. He lowered his MPK and took a few steps forward, thinking: *Did he commit suicide? Where's the gun?*

At that instant, a gunshot rang out from behind him, and a speeding slug ripped through Castor's last thought, painting the beige wall on the opposite side of the bullet's entry-wound a slightly darker color, thus ending his time on this plane of existence.

* * * *

Peter stared past a smoking revolver at the dead 'detective' lying just inside the front door, still clutching the wicked-looking sub-machine gun in a death grip. Then he walked eight steps into the kitchen, peeking around the corner; the back door stood open and the second detective lay on the floor, his face a bloody mess. The trap had worked perfectly.

I can't believe that I pulled that one off.

"Bravo, Petey."

Peter whirled around to see Seth; and what did Peter see upon his pale face? *A smile.*

"That shotgun thing was *brilliant.* A perfect ten for sure." Seth said appraisingly.

"*Go to Hell,* Seth."

"Come again?"

Peter felt all his hate and anger and loathing well up at once; an acidic ball of red frenzy that shook the very foundation of his being. "I said *go...to...Hell.*"

Seth shook his head, and approached Peter; still smiling. “Petey. *Petey.* I thought we were past all this. I thought we had an understanding.” He narrowed his black eyes. “I...have...the power.” He said, poking Peter in the chest with each delivery, to emphasize his point.

Peter cocked back his fist and swung with all the strength he could muster, hitting Seth squarely in the jaw. The result was quite similar to the reaction one gets when ice-cold water is run over a glass dish freshly out of the oven; Seth shattered into a million cackling shards.

YOU CAN’T HURT ME, PETEY. Seth’s voice boomed from behind Peter’s eyes.

The Whooptolly rematerialized again in front of his host. “I am not of this world, and thus, in this world I cannot die.” Maddening laughter filled Peter’s mind once more.

Peter grabbed Seth by the throat and held him firmly in place.

“What are you gonna do, huh? JUST WHAT THE HELL ARE YOU GONNA DO?” Seth roared defiantly, laughing like the mad thing that he was.

Peter closed his eyes and concentrated. He plucked a sound out of the darkness of his mind; a soft shirring sound.

Seth suddenly started to thrash in his grip. "What the shit?! No!"

Sanity and insanity took each other by the arm and began to dance; the sound of waves became stronger in Peter's mind as the tear began to grow, a brilliant white line that when touched, opened to the land of madness.

"Peter, please! Don't do this!" Seth cried pathetically, pleading for the first time in his long existence. "I like it here!"

Peter opened his eyes and perceived the line. "Time to go home."

"NO!!!"

Seth was shoved backward into the fissure between worlds with a violent thrust and there was a sound, similar to that of silk tearing, before that pale demon was ripped back into the world of the Whooptolly.

"Bye bye now." Peter said quietly into the still air (air that smelled of gunpowder and hope intermingled). "Don't forget to write."

After placing the revolver in the hand of the deceased elder (to help convey a picture of double-murder/suicide) Peter stepped over the body of Pollux, taking care not to step in blood, and walked out the back door. He hopped a few fences, dodged a very mean-looking German Shepherd (deja-vu), and after a few blocks of hurried walking (he could hear sirens in the distance; a neighbor must have heard the shots and called 911) he got into his Camaro and started the engine.

Finally free.

- -

Behind the Looking-Glass

After a long, peacefully quiet ride through the city streets, Peter finally pulled into his assigned parking space: 32A. He killed the engine and let out a long breath of bottled relief.

Home sweet home.

After retrieving his Beretta and locking the car, Peter made his way through the maze of vehicles and to the main building. A black cat ran past him as he made a beeline for the stairs, but it didn't phase him in the least; he was too happy to think about petty superstition.

Jeremy was sitting on the couch, watching the Discovery Channel and smoking a bowl out of his 'bing.' He raised an index and middle finger in lazy gesture of greeting (peace, man) as Peter stepped through the door.

"Sup, pothead." Peter said, sitting down on the couch next to his roommate; his only friend in the world.

"Nothin'. I was just watching some Cheetah chew the shit out of an antel-" His sentence was cut short as Peter plucked the small bong and lighter out of his hands, then to Jeremy's surprise, lit the bowl and took a long draw, filling the chamber until it became thick with yellow smoke.

Peter grabbed the glass handle on the side of the bowl and slid it out of its tube, like he had seen his friend do before, allowing air to enter and clear the chamber. Pungent smoke shot into Peter's lungs, setting them aflame with all the intensity of a blast furnace, and making it seem as if someone had inflated his chest to four times its original size; he tried to hold it in like he had seen Jeremy do with such ease on several occasions, but he could only manage a few short seconds before it exploded out in an expansive gray plume. He coughed like he had never coughed before, not able to catch his breath through all the burning in his chest.

Oh God, I'm dying. He thought in a panic, feeling a sudden body-rush of heat, and beads of sweat broke out on his forehead.

Jeremy was, at this point, rolling with laughter. "Are you *okay?* You took a straight *champion* of a hit there, bro."

"I...can't...breathe." Peter gasped, tears rolling from his eyes.

"Oh, don't worry, you'll be alright. It's like that the first time; your lungs will eventually adapt. Just keep taking steady breaths."

Peter tried to ignore the irritation in the back of his throat that made him want to continue coughing; forcing himself to do as his friend, the expert stoner, told him to. After a few minutes the pressure started to subside, and his breathing once again developed some semblance of a regular pattern.

Jeremy went into the kitchen, and came back with two ice-cold colas in hand, giving one of them to Peter. "Here you go, killer. This ought to help."

Peter flinched at the unknowing reference to his profession, then popped open the tab on the soda. The resulting *hiss* caused by escaping carbonation was like music to his ears; he could not remember having ever felt so *thirsty.* He greedily chugged half the soda, then emitted a moderate belch.

Jeremy jokingly wiped away a non-existent tear. "I'm so proud."

Peter laughed. It seemed like the funniest thing he had ever heard anyone say before in his entire life. He laughed deeply, from the bottom of his stomach (which would eventually start to ache from the strain), and new tears rolled down his cheeks. The high had enveloped him like a warm, fuzzy blanket, and it felt like there was an itch (but not the unpleasantness, just that involuntary feeling) hiding behind his face, making him grin without reason.

Maybe that's why Seth grins so much. Peter thought to himself, bursting into another fit of chortling laughter. *Maybe he was rockin' the ganja, too.*

Five hours, four bong hits, eight sodas, a box of twinkies, and three grande microwavable burritos later, Peter was feeling pretty good. Nah, better than that. He was higher than skydiving hippie; *lifted* was a more accurate description of what he was feeling.

"Look, all I'm saying is that I think drugs have done some good things for people over the years." Jeremy was dishing out another one of his fascinating spiels.

"Yeah. Me too, man." Peter said, feeling as if he were speaking through a mouthful of cotton.

Jeremy held out a fist and bumped knuckles with his inebriated roommate. "Anyone who says differently should go back to wherever-the-hell it is that they live, take all their CDs, tapes, and records, and just *burn* them."

"Why?" Peter asked with genuine curiosity.

"Why? I'll tell ya' why: because all those musicians who made that music that inspired us and so many people over the years..." He paused dramatically. "Were high as fuck."

At some point the high broke into a visual realm; Peter started to notice tracers and flashes of color that made him both shudder and smile involuntarily. After another hour of that, he was tired and feeling a bit queasy from all the junk food he had voraciously consumed while stricken with a severe case of the 'munchies.'

"I think I'm gonna crash."

Jeremy nodded. "Okay, buddy. Night." Then, after a moment, "Hey man, I had a lot of fun tonight."

Peter smiled, once again thinking to himself how good it was to have a friend. "Me too. Night."

Right before Peter slipped into bed, an alarm went off in his head; he could not make out the details, for the pot had fogged that little bit of clairvoyance that he possessed, but he was left with an ominous feeling. He unlocked his lock-box, pulled out the Beretta, popped in a loaded clip, and tucked it under his pillow.

There.

As Peter drifted off to sleep he heard his mental alarm again, only this time softer; the ominous feeling (like the eerie calm before a truly terrible storm) once again embraced him as unconsciousness rolled over like a wave...and he dreamed.

Peter dreamed of an unending sea, in a world of never ending twilight. Helpless souls (lost vagrants from other worlds both parallel and crossing) filled the waters, screaming in agony as the Whooptollies punctured their floating bodies with wicked tridents from the air and from their boats; the vessels, made of flesh and broken bones tied together with sinew, ruthlessly swept aside anything in their path, leaving behind a trail of blood and agony.

Peter dreamed of a massive castle on a island in the center of that twilight world, where sat the throne of the king of the Whooptollies. He also dreamed that Seth sat upon that throne, holding the dripping head of one of his brethren; the former king.

He dreamed that Seth smiled at him with that everlasting smile.

Peter awoke in a cold sweat; crying from the next room and his own ragged breathing were the only sounds that were audible. He looked at the digital clock next to his bed, it's LED display reading 3:13 AM, and got out of bed, opening the door; a dark silhouette was visible sitting on the couch in the living room, shoulders shaking with each racking sob.

Peter snapped on the lamp that sat on a table next to his favorite armchair, which emitted a soft glow throughout the room, and revealed the troubled look on his friend's face. "What's wrong, Jeremy?" He sat down next to his friend on the couch.

"I had a bad dream...about you."

Peter stiffened; a cold knot started to form in the pit of his stomach. "Oh? What about?"

Jeremy looked into Peter's eyes, fresh tears spilling down his cheeks. "I dreamed of a bad man with black hair and black eyes, and an evil smile; he gave me a knife, and he told me to kill you." He wiped the moisture from his cheeks to make room for fresh streams. "In my dream, I *wanted* to, Peter. *I would have been glad to do it.*"

Peter put a hand on his friend's shoulder, in order to help comfort him; he himself was, in fact, more frightened than ever. "It was just a dream. I wouldn't worry too much about it."

Jeremy shook his head. "No Peter, it wasn't just a dream. When I woke up, I was standing in the hallway, holding this." He reached beside him, and pulled out a knife that Peter hadn't noticed; it was thin and made of what looked like black glass, curving slightly and tapering down to a needle point. "What the hell is going on?"

The cold knot that had started to form in Peter's stomach snowballed into a void of icy dread. "Wait here." He got up from the couch and started to walk to Jeremy's room, but turned before he completed the journey. "And I mean *don't move.*"

Jeremy nodded.

Peter went into his friend's room, glanced around at the chaos within, and then spotted what he was looking for; the full length mirror with which Jeremy used to inspect himself daily before venturing into the world. He grabbed it and dragged it into the living room. "Do you have any more mirrors?"

Jeremy was red-eyed and confused, but for once, it wasn't because of the pot. "What?"

"Mirrors! Do you have any more mirrors?!" Peter yelled.

"Um, in the bathroom; the medicine cabinet is the only other one."

"Break it." Peter said, dragging the large mirror into his bedroom. He heard glass shattering as he positioned the full-length next to the one of similar size and shape that he had in his own room.

Jeremy came in a moment later. "Again I find myself asking you, what the hell is going on, Peter?"

Peter turned to his friend with a heavy heart. "I never meant to get you involved in this, Jeremy, I swear, but right now your life is in danger."

"What the shit, why?"

"Because you're the only thing he can use against me."

"Who?"

Peter sighed. "The man that you saw in your dream, but he's not really a man, not like us; he's more like the monsters that we tell our children don't exist. He calls himself Seth, but that's not his real name either." *The real Seth was a good man.*

Jeremy shook his head, not in disbelief, but because he was overwhelmed. "What do we do, Peter?"

Peter once again put his hand on Jeremy's shoulder. "I need you to listen carefully and not say anything. Is that clear?"

Jeremy nodded.

"Okay. In a minute or two, I'm going to disappear. Ten seconds after I do, I need you to break that mirror." He pointed at the full-length closest to the bathroom. "After that, I need you to take my car somewhere, preferably out-of-town, and wait for me to call you on your cell." He was silent for a moment. "If I don't call...then I'm dead. If you don't get a call, don't come back to town."

Jeremy was very pale. "Is this shit for real?"

"I wish it wasn't."

"Jeremy paused for a moment, then nodded. "Okay. Ten seconds after you disappear, take the car and get the hell out of Dodge. Wait for your call. If you don't call, change my name to Francesco and cut an album." Tears started to well in his eyes. "You'd better call, man."

Peter was silent; he stared into the mirror, listening for the sound of madness. The shirring sound of doom. After a moment, the sound of the sea filled his ears, and he began to perceive the line; the mirror's consistency became less like glass and more like water, shimmering and rippling. A doorway between the worlds. Peter turned and gave his friend one last parting nod, then he did as Alice had done so many years ago; Peter stepped through the looking-glass and into the world beyond.

Jeremy watched, completely sober, as his friend stepped into a mirror and vanished. As he was told, he waited ten seconds (one-one-thousand, two-one-thousand...) then smashed the reflective glass with the heel of one of his shoes, taking care to make sure there were no large pieces left.

Then, also as he was told, he grabbed Peter's keys and, as the saying goes, 'got the hell out of Dodge.'"

- -

The World of the Whooptolly

Peter piloted the small boat across the waters, protected by the line.

He had closed his eyes while stepping through the full-length mirror in his bedroom, and had opened them again in a world that was not like the one he remembered visiting years before. The world of the Whooptolly was no longer a place of beauty, it was a place of twilight and death; it was Hell.

Where once there was a great gathering of seafaring souls that lived their life in peace, fishing and living off the vast oceans, there now was only suffering; the wreckage of houseboats numbering in the hundreds of thousands littered the waters as far as the eye could perceive. The sea was filled with those thrashing souls, who cried out to the heavens for sympathy from their afflictions; some cursed God with bitter tongues of venomous blasphemy, cursed their ancestor's seed that had begotten them for the pain of their life, and cursed themselves for not dying sooner. Even the very totality of the universe did these poor souls curse while they thrashed in those perilous waters. They clawed over each other, drowning one another in panic-driven mania; a chaotic frenzy to stay above the icy waters as screams of rage and futility filled the salty air.

Some of the souls used their fallen neighbors as flotation devices to escape the pull of the deep; the inevitable death that awaited them all, if not the one dealt by the hands of the dreadful Whooptolly.

The Whooptollies, with their leathery wings and their grinning faces of malignant humor, swooped to and fro in kamikaze flights, stabbing at the helpless souls in the water with rusty tridents and cackling with glee. Some of the demons flew down low, scooping up a victim from time to time, taking them high into the air and dropping them, or sometimes just gnawing at their faces and limbs until nothing identifiable remained, before releasing them unto the raging waters below. Peter feared not the Whooptollies in flight, for he was protected by the jealousy of their ruler, who wanted Peter for himself; not to mention that he could command the line, and Shear the tear.

He peered through the surface of the murky water and saw the bodies of those that the sea had overcome. The gases released from their eternally rotting corpses were like so many sighs of the undead, sunk deep within the loathsome slime of eternity.

One of these wretched souls raised his slime-covered head from the waters as Peter's vessel passed, and cried out, "What manner of man are ye, to have come upon this forsaken place without fear? Doth not death by the hands of the evil ones concern ye?"

Peter slowed the vessel's pace with but a thought, and spoke in the manner of speech presented to him. "I am one who comes seeking vengeance against the unholy king of this realm, the evil one who commands those of whom you speak. Death be not a worry of mine, but if you question my manner, then I will yours. What manner of man are *you*, to have come to be in such a loathsome place and resign yourself to the evils wherein? To allow yourself to be swept away by the madness of this sea without fight. I ask, if you give in to that which afflicts you, what manner of man are you?"

The soul, brought to shame by Peter's words, said

no more of his own, but sank once again into the oily waters.

Peter again resumed his journey toward the kingdom that lay in the center of the watery world, navigating his small vessel upon the waves with a fixity of resolve that could not be wavered by the devil himself.

Funny, for is it not the devil whom I seek to confront now, to wage battle?

At times, the twilight sky darkened with fiery clouds, and burning brimstone rained down from the heavens above onto the poor souls of the sea, causing the very waters to boil; the tortured souls wailed relentlessly as they all but cooked in the roiling sea.

Peter navigated the deathly broth unsinged, ever progressing toward that grinning madman that had lived inside him for so many years, whispering into his ear and influencing his life. When Seth's castle became visible in the distance, standing in all its unholy glory, Peter was not fearful; he was like stone.

A pissed-off stone.

- -

The Sentry

The castle of the Mad King loomed before Peter, a monstrous architecture of lunacy and chaos stretching into the fiery clouds. It was built on the only piece of land in the entire Whooptolly world, and of the same black glass as the knife that Jeremy had showed him, with several hundred, if not thousands of branching towers that tapered to needlepoint spires.

Peter stood beside his vessel upon the shores of madness, staring at the evil epitome of Seth's reign in this world, and feeling a bit transfixed by sheer size of it. Never in his life had he seen such a structure, so utterly massive as to encompass the whole of his mind such as this one did; it warped the perception, as madness often does, and would have set any normal man upon his knees cowering, his sanity shattered.

Compensating for something, Seth?

Peter trekked across the hard, lifeless ground

toward the tower of madness, readying himself for the inevitable conflict that was to come; Seth may not have been able to harm him in the other world, but here he was King, and he was pissed about being sent home. Shielding himself from the occasional shower of brimstone, Peter made his way toward the castle.

When Peter came within sight of yonder castle doors, he was greeted by an ogre who stood guard. Twice the size of Peter's height was he, with arms as thick as tree trunks, and scaly green skin covered with living moss and skittering insects. He wore a cloth tied between his legs, an iron hoop through the septum of his flat, piggish nose, and a crude necklace made of what appeared to be human skulls. He hefted in his hands a giant quarterstaff, made of dark glazed wood.

"Ye shall not pass, outworlder." The creature spoke in a rough, gritty tone. "I am Sentry to this place of evil, and my king does not allow visitors."

Peter gave the creature a dismissive look. "The rules don't apply to me, Tiny, I'm from California."

The ogre regarded him with large confused eyes. "Ye shall not pass." It repeated; unsure of itself.

Peter took a step forward. "I heard *you*, did you hear *me*? I don't care!!" He roared at the beast, and was a little surprised to see it flinch; it surprised him, but he felt something else as well, something..."If you don't move the hell out of my way, I'm going to have to get *epic* on your ass. You hear me, Tiny? MOVE!!"

The ogre didn't move; it only stared at him with those dark eyes. "Strange little thing." It finally said, then lifted its giant staff, swinging it in a deadly two-handed arc.

Peter dodged the blow effortlessly, letting himself melt with the sound of rushing water; the shirring sound. He regained his feet as the ogre caught balance, ready to swing again, and he unsheathed the item that he had brought with him through the mirror from the other side: the glass dagger. He readied the weapon in his hand as the ogre charged at him, swinging wildly. Peter ducked, feeling the wood whistle past his head, and dove at the creature's passing leg, slashing savagely at its Achilles tendon; vile, black blood spilled onto the ground as the ogre involuntarily dropped to one knee, and Peter repeated similar process on the creature's other heel, releasing another dark spray of lifeblood. Once finished with the heels, Peter continued to dance the cutting song; severing the four tendons behind the knees, puncturing the femoral arteries, and getting 'western' by performing a good old-fashioned ogre castration.

The creature screamed and thrashed its arms, trying desperately to swat at the small creature that was hurting it so *badly*, but to no avail. It lay there, shuddering and bloody, as Peter finished his work down below, then jumped onto the creature's back.

"I told you to move, Tiny, but look at you now, lying there, bleeding and shit!!" Peter stood for a moment, rising and falling with the ogre's quickening breath, and thought to himself, *Did I really just do that?* He looked down at his hands, covered in blackened gore. *I guess I'd better finish, this is by far my best work.* He stepped across the creature's massive back, leaned down, and severed the enormous jugular vein, erupting an explosive flow of oozing blackness onto the baked ground. The ogre made a wet, strangling sound and convulsed once...twice...then lay still forevermore.

Peter wiped the blade clean on the creature's flesh, then jumped down from its back and walked up to the castle doors. A skinny Whooptolly stood off to the side, holding its rusty trident with mouth agape, having just witnessed a human kill the Sentry without receiving so much as a single scratch.

Peter regarded the creature with hostile eyes. "What the hell are *you* looking at?

The Whooptolly let out a frightened screech, and retreated to the skies in a flurry of flapping wings.

"That's right, fly away!! Go tell your buddies!! Petey's come to *play*!!" He yelled after it, flipping it the 'bird.'

Peter then walked the rest of the way up to the massive doors and pulled on the handles...but they wouldn't budge.

"Are you serious?" Peter stepped back from the doors and looked up; yelling to the heavens. "Did you really think that I would come from another world, paddle my ass across the simmering soul gumbo, kill your guard dog, and then just leave because the *door's locked?!"* He bought his attention to the doors, focusing all his anger on them, and then let the line *rip*. The double doors exploded inward into a billion tiny wooden splinters with a sound that reminded Peter of water crashing in your ears when you cannonball into a swimming pool.

He stepped through the threshold, feeling that feeling he felt when the ogre flinched, and recognized it for what it was: power.

"Lucy!!!" He called into the echoing corridor. "I'm

home!!!

And you've got some serious splainin' to do.

- -

Tweedle-Dee and Tweedle-Dum

As Peter crossed the large room (which now lay littered with so many splinters), looking at the odd statues of grotesque creatures that adorned the chamber with disgust while passing, he realized that he was being watched; watched not by Seth's ever-gazing sight (he had felt that upon entering this world), but by something closer, in the room with him.

"Come out, come out, wherever you are!!" He called out into the seemingly empty space.

From the far end of the great room, two figures appeared from the shadows, striding forth with the grace of confidence and skill; as they neared, Peter saw that they were twin Whooptollies, though they were wingless. They each wore wide-brimmed hats, fastened to their heads with hide chinstraps, and long, regally-decorated coats that were fastened down the front with loops and bone toggles; they had total of eight arms between the two of them, each with two separate sets, and upon their many hands they wore long claws that tapered to fine points.

They considered him with large, ovate eyes that were full of somber intelligence. He could feel their minds attempting to probe his own, though they were unable to divide the line.

The Whooptolly on the left spoke to its companion in a voice that was reminiscent of Yoda from *Star Wars*. "How has this come to be? How has this come to pass? This human be come, from the world outside the glass."

Then his companion answered in like voice. "I know how, my brother, though I know not why; this human is strong, and calls upon the line."

The eyes of the first widened in understanding. "Ah, the line, the power of the light; if he could control it, that would be a sight."

Peter laughed at the creatures, and joined their rhyme. "Behold Alice, from the darkness has come; the comic relief of Tweedle-dee and Tweedle-dum."

The Tweedles showed no emotion. Tweedle-dee addressed his brethren. "Look, brother, he mocks us, what shall we do? He trespasses upon us, and our kind he hath already slew."

"Teach him a lesson; rip flesh, and with claws run him through." Tweedle-dum answered. "That is our purpose which we shall do.

Peter shook his head, smiling. "I'm not much of a poet, but I have one more that's just for you two." He stated, listening to waves build while holding the line in his mind. "Step aside wretched demons, turn tail as if belly be yellow; before I break my foot off in your ass, like I did that tall, ugly fellow."

That got the Tweedle blood flowing; they were apparently fond of the Sentry.

"Time to show aggression." Dee said, scowling with thin, bloodless lips.

"Teach him a lesson." Dum replied in mirror-like fashion.

Tweedle-dee and Tweedle-dum unfastened the toggles on their long coats, each motion by one mirrored by the other in perfect accord; they tossed their coats and hats aside, revealing to Peter their lithe, muscular torsos and black-haired top-knots. Their forms were the bodies of acrobats.

They proved this assumption to be true as they performed a stunning fusillade of end-over-end flips and cartwheels that would have put Olympic Tumblers to shame, and came to rest mere feet away from where Peter stood; their every motion so perfectly timed to one another that Peter believed they must be of one mind.

Their feet shifted back and forth in a fluid, rhythmic dance, reminding Peter of *Capoeira,* and their muscles rippled in eerie unison; he held onto the line, letting it build until it seeped into his pores and permeated his very being, until he felt as if he would explode.

Tweedle-dee attacked first with quick slashes of his claws that would have left Peter headless had he not shifted to the side, and the Tweedle-dum attacked in a manner that was perfectly symmetrical, causing Peter to have to painfully contort his body in order to dodge the deadly points.

Quick little bastards, ain'tcha? Peter thought, springing backward from another flurry of needlepoint claws, and laid his hands on the stone floor in a half crouch, panting. "I hate to break a sweat." He let the power of the line trickle into his hands, and they tingled with heat.

The floor in front of the twins erupted in a stone shower, and the concussive force of the blast blew them into the air; Peter let loose the rest of the line in a flat sheet of crackling energy that swept through the airborne creatures in mid-flight.

Tweedle-dee and Tweedle-dum fell to the stone floor several yards away from their lift-off point, twitching and seizing erratically, their flesh smoking.

Not mirror-matching now, are you? Peter looked from the dying Whooptolly brothers to the impressive stone steps that ascended the wall nearest him. *Up, up, and away; here comes Petey boy to save the day.*

- -

Tomb Raider

Peter climbed the steps to the next level in the tower of madness, counting 133 steps before reaching the last, and passed through the corridor beyond. Oil paintings decorated the long hallway on both sides, depicting scenes of violence and images that disturbed the senses.

He paused to study one of the paintings. It portrayed a group of nude men and women who had just landed a vessel upon the shores of madness, brandishing crude, jagged scythes; their anger and outrage was prominent on their contorted faces and mid-step bodies, forever frozen in time in an attempt to storm the approaching Whooptolly. The demons rushed the beached vessel with like hatred for their quarry, both flying and wingless, like the Tweedles; and among their ranks was a hideous creature that Peter could only describe as the 'death worm'.

It had a number of short, misshapen legs

underneath a lump of a head that displayed several rows of razor sharp teeth, and eyes that were perched on the ends of long, vein-covered stalks; tentacles emerged from its wide mouth amid the rows of teeth, searching for seafaring flesh to yank into its maws. Its dark skin looked shiny in the still twilight, and Peter just *knew* that its tail made a vile squishing sound as it crept forward, like it was filled with some sort of jelly, or perhaps the half-coagulated blood of its partially digested victims.

Above this still scene of two warring sides, the image of Seth, sitting upon a crimson cloud, cheerfully watching the events unfold below him as he regally sipped from a glass that may have been filled with dark wine, or perhaps blood. On the cloud beside Seth sat a young, white-haired Whooptolly with black wings, not bat-like, like other Whooptollies, but comprised of feathers in the shade of midnight; Peter wondered who the demon was, to be so allowed to sit with the Mad King.

He continued down the hallway until he came upon a piece of art that was not a painting, but instead, a scripture engraved in a slab of white ivory. It read:

Behold the tomb of Mimir the Wise.

All of the worlds, and all of their glories
Did he gaze upon with his eyes.
Here he shall remain, unable to be awoken,
For the door shall not open
With out the utterance; 'No sooner Spoken than Broken.'

Peter stared at the engraving, mystified. "No sooner spoken than broken."

He thought about it. *No sooner spoken than broken. What breaks when you say it?* The answer hit him with a burst of neurological energy that stemmed from the area of the brain that was devoted to memory; he had heard the riddle long ago, when he was still in school. It was Jeremy who had come up to him one day and asked the riddle (*betcha' can't guess this one!*), and when Peter gave up Jeremy had smiled triumphantly, saying-

"Silence."

There was a harsh, grating sound as a five-foot section of wall (with the engraving in the center) recessed, then slid out of view to reveal a winding staircase that lead downward into blackness; there was a single, blue-flamed torch in a holder at the top of the steep, earthen steps.

Peter lifted the torch out of its holder, pausing for

a moment to ponder the odd flame, then held it over the blackened pit, peering into its depths; he could not see the bottom, for the unnatural torchlight could not penetrate the nearly tangible darkness, but he could tell that it descended much farther down than just back to the first floor of the tower.

Well, what to do? Peter asked himself as he stared into the opening. *Should I stay or should I go?* The decision was clear from the start, he was going; he just felt the need to feign a debate of thought, for the sake of argument and to prepare himself. Using the line so much was taxing; he felt as if he had just run a mile. Shaking his head to clear his thoughts, Peter took a deep breath, then released it, and started to descend the staircase that had been carved into the hard-packed earth.

He did not attempt to count the steps, he only descended silently into the darkness; as he did, the air became musty, and the walls became slick with moisture. Down and down did Peter descend into the tomb of Mimir, unknowing of what he might find at the end of the journey; when he reached the bottom he could hear the sound of trickling water.

At the bottom of the stairs, he found a doorway that opened into a small room that had no doors or windows, at the center of which lay a ornately-carved stone pedestal; on the pedestal sat the severed head of a middle-aged seafaring man.

Peter stepped closer to the pedestal to get a better look; when he came within range where he could have reached out his hand and touched it, something happened that caused him to jump back, startled.

The head had stretched open its mouth in a wide, gaping yawn, then opened its eyes, blinking several times in the brightness of the torchlight. “Welcome, outworlder.” It said in a voice that was raspy with disuse. “I expected thee would come.”

Peter stared at the head in pure stupefied fascination. “I know I should be past little odd things like this, but wow.” He chuckled. “A talking head.”

“I am called Mimir.” It pronounced the name *meemer.*

“Mimir the Wise?”

Mimir’s face gave a thoughtful expression. “Aye. They called me that once.” A moment of silence. “Yes…long ago, when I was advisor to the King of Whooptollies, Verucian, who reigned before the evil Seth.” It spat the grinning devil’s name out with distaste. “Verucian was a peaceful king, who only wanted peace with the sea people; Seth is a vicious thing, full of hate and wrath, who has poisoned this once peaceful world."

"How is it possible that Seth has done such a thing when I sent him here only a day before?"

"Seth did not destroy our world in a day." Mimir stated flatly. "Seth's reign has lasted longer than ten-thousand days." Upon seeing Peter's shocked expression, he continued. "Do you think that time flows equally throughout the universe? It does not; time is just another dimension that is perceived, and in each world that strand flows arbitrarily."

Peter was silent for a gravid moment. A question rose in the back of his mind and tried desperately to claw its way to the surface; he voiced his inquiry when it reached the apex of that climb. "If I were to return to my world after my business in this one is finished, how much time will have passed?"

"There is no definite way to tell. You could end up in the same time as when you left, or you could end stepping through to the empty space that was your world before creation; theoretical physics is not an exact science, so you just never really *know*."

Peter thought about the implications of this revelation. When he was finished with his task in this world, even if he did survive to travel back to his own, there was a definite possibility that it would not be the same world he had left. He realized that there was no turning back; no hope of a return to normalcy.

"Well, I guess there's no going home then."

Mimir gave him a guarded look. "And what would you do in *this* world of cruelty, outworlder?"

Peter shrugged. "When in Rome, do as the Romans do; I'm going to kill the King."

"A worthy feat. You will have much obstruction in your path."

Peter smiled. "I'll be fine, I walk the line."

Mimir was silent for a moment before speaking. "I have weighed the good and the bad that can arise in this, and have come to this conclusion: whether or not you succeed in this venture of yours, in my tomb I shall remain. I will help you, outworlder, though all I can offer is knowledge."

"I would take the knowledge and put it to good use, and be thankful for it."

"Very well," Mimir replied. "You will face three adversaries before your confrontation with the Dark King. The first is of no concern, if you have a sound mind, for he is Coeus the Riddler, and he doth battle with words."

Peter chortled. "That doesn't sound very dangerous."

"Perhaps, but if you fail his test, you will never pass." Mimir warned. "The second adversary you face will be Mnemosyne (nem-o-see-nay), a siren who will cause you false visions. Beware when you begin to doubt what you see, for it may very well be the death of you."

"I'll keep that in mind."

"The last adversary you will face before the King himself is the Titan, the King's second in power and personal bodyguard."

"He wouldn't happened to be the black-winged fellow in that painting upstairs, would he?" Peter asked.

"The very same."

"Why is he called the Titan? He doesn't look all that tough."

"They call him Titan because he too can control the power of the line."

"Oh." *I had to ask, didn't I?*

Mimir paused, the asked, "Has your resolve been wavered?"

Peter shook his head. "Not in the least."

"Then farewell, outworlder, and good luck to you."

- -

Riddle Me This

Peter climbed the earthen steps to the hallway above, and once at the top, he replaced the unnatural torch and spoke the answer to the tomb's riddle once more, closing the door so that no unintelligent beast could enter and ravage the helpless Mimir. He proceeded further down the hallway of Whooptolly art to a t-section, took a left turn (*take the left because the right way is wrong)*, and continued until he came upon a plain wooden door, roughly standard in size when compared to those found in his own world; the knob turned freely, and he let the door swing open.

He stepped through the doorway into the darkened room beyond, and the door snapped shut behind him; he was left trapped on a ledge no more that ten feet wide before it abruptly dropped into impenetrable blackness. Peter surveyed the room as his eyes adjusted, though it was so massive that, apart from the area with the door as well as the area he stood on, he could see no other traces of floors, walls, or ceiling; it was as if he was a part of a painting that was only semi-finished, and painted on a black canvas instead of white.

A voice rang out from somewhere in the darkness of the canvas. “So you are the one who hath solved the riddle of the tomb?”

Peter, alarmed, called onto the line, eyes darting for the source of the voice in the thick blackness. “In the flesh.” Peter answered. “Now show yourself! I like to look the person I’m speaking to in the eye.”

The voice chuckled. “I shall, but why don’t you first ease your grip on that power that you wield so enthusiastically; I assure you there is no need for that here.”

Peter shook his head. “You really expect me to believe that? If you’re with *them*, then you’re the enemy, and I don’t trust the enemy.”

“I am not like the mass of brutish creatures that you have seen, those I am ashamed to call my brethren, for I am an educated soul; I loathe the shedding of blood, and choose to commence my battles with words. I will show a gesture of good faith by revealing myself, if you will but lessen your grip a bit.”

“Okay, I can deal with that.” *If he tries anything,*

I'll fry him. Peter let the power of the line slip through his mental fingers like so much sand, until only a small trickle was left.

Almost immediately after, an ancient-looking man with a white beard and a long, flowing gray robe shimmered into view; he stood perhaps twenty yards away atop a floating square of what appeared to be smoky pyrex, leaning slightly on a staff that was made of the ever-popular black glass of the Whooptolly world. The tip of the glass staff, much thicker than the shaft and bulbous in shape, glowed with an intense blue light that was of the same shade as the unnatural torch he had found earlier.

Jesus, he looks like a member of a druidic ZZ-Top cover band.

"Okay, so how does this word battle work, Billy?" Peter asked. "Name-calling? Momma' jokes? Game of scrabble? What?"

The ancient man drew his brows together in confusion. "We shall riddle."

"Oh yeah, that's right. 'Cuz you're Coeus the riddler."

Coeus nodded. "That's correct. I will ask you riddles, which you will answer with truth; for every correct answer you will be brought closer to the other end of the room, and to the next level of the castle." A smoky glass square, like the one the old man stood upon, appeared next to the ledge directly in front of where Peter stood.

"And if I answer incorrectly?" *As if I have to ask.*

Coeus smiled. "If you should answer a single riddle incorrectly, then the square will vanish and you will fall through blackness for the span of an eternity."

Oh, well that's nice. Peter thought. "I guess I don't really have much of a choice other than to answer them correctly. Do I get a warm-up question?"

Coeus shook his head. "The riddle of the tomb was as much practice as I'll allow."

"Well, shit...where do I sign up?"

The old man gestured to the glass square.

Peter took a deep breath, mentally preparing himself much the same way as he would if he were about to leap out of an airplane knowing that a blind man had packed his chute (*time to step up to the plate*), then he boarded the glass square; for a horrifying moment, he thought that he had been duped and would fall into the blackness without so much as a single answered riddle, but it was only a momentary sinking of about an inch before the platform steadied itself.

The riddling commenced.

"Everyone sees me without noticing me, for what is beyond is what he or she seeks." Coeus said, then fell silent, apparently finished.

Peter thought hard. *They see it without noticing, looking at something beyond it.* Peter could not fathom an immediate answer to the riddle, and became quickly panicked. *Shit! I don't want to die because of a riddle, and especially not the first one I'm asked!* He had a sudden urge to consume the old man with the power of the line, and to Coeus' alarm he actually filled himself with it before suppressing the desire, instead diverting it upward, hoping that it might help grease the wheels of his mind a little. When the warm sensation of the line collided with his brain tissue, an immediate explosion of thought filled his mind like a fusion-bomb, and the riddle's elusive answer flew from Peter's lips like an involuntary expulsion of breath caused by a powerful gut-punch. "Window!"

Coeus, who had begun smiling when he first sensed Peter's panic, now gave an expression of surprised dismay. "That's correct."

The glass platform on which Peter stood shifted away from the stone ledge, coming to rest at a precarious wobble nearly twenty feet from its original starting position, then it leveled out once more.

"That was fun." Peter stated sarcastically. "Almost like Disneyland, but with all the excitement of impending death."

Coeus paid no attention to these comments, only continued with another riddle. "I pass before the sun, yet make no shadow."

Peter once again used the power of the line to fuel his mind, and the answer once again spewed forth from his unsuspecting lips. "The wind."

Coeus once again nodded, and the platform once again moved another twenty or so feet. Thus was how the battle of words was played out; the riddle, the answer, the nod, the flight of the square.

Not born, but from a Mother's body drawn,
I hang until half of me is gone.
I sleep in a cave until I grow old,
Then I'm valued for my hardened gold.

"Cheese."

Lovely and round,
I shine with pale light;

Grown in the darkness,
A lady's delight.

"A pearl."

My thunder comes before the lightning
My lightning comes before the clouds
My rain dries all the the land it touches.

"A volcano."

Look at me
I can bring a smile to your face
A tear to your eye
Or a thought to your mind
But I can't be seen.

"Memory."

A skin have I
More eyes than one
I can be very nice
When I am done.

"A potato."

I'm as small as an ant
And as big as a whale
I'll dance to the music
Though I can't hear
I'm as slow as a snail
But from me you just can't run.

"Shadow."

I am not alive, yet I grow
I don't have lungs, but I need air
I don't have a mouth, yet I must be fed.

"Fire."

Peter, balancing on the glass platform as it made its unsteady journey, spotted the stone ledge that held the exit door (the other side of the unfinished painting) in the distance.

Coeus, who had been so cheerful at the start of the test, was visibly becoming vexed as Peter answered riddle after riddle correctly; he had been expecting failure, had been *counting* on failure, and the turn of events disturbed him deeply. If the human succeeded, it would surely cause him death by the hand of his King, but Coeus was a being who respected both knowledge and the power of words, and would play the game that he started, which was played by the rules that he himself created. If the human won, then so be it.

I build up castles
I tear down mountains
I make some folks blind
And I help others to see.

"Sand."

Three lives have I:
Gentle enough to soothe the skin
Light enough to caress the sky
Hard enough to split rocks.

"Water."

Different lights do make me strange
Thus into different sizes will I change.

"Eye pupils."

I am deaf, dumb, and blind
Yet I always tell the truth.

"A mirror."

At night they come without being fetched
And by day they are lost without being stolen.

"The stars."

I walk upon four legs in the morning.
And two legs in the afternoon.
During the evening, I walk upon three.

"A human." Crawls on all fours during infancy, walks on two in his middle years, and walks aided by a cane in his last years.

Coeus looked at Peter with sad eyes. "You have but one to go, and the battle is done."

Peter beckoned with his hands in a 'bring it on' gesture. "Fire away."

Coeus gave one last attempt.

I am greater than God
I am more evil than the Morning Star
I can be found where anything cannot
Dead men feast on me
If a living man eats me, he'll die.

Peter hesitated. He did not need the power of the line to answer this riddle, for he had heard it once before from his dearest friend, but he had said 'Devil' instead of 'Morning Star.' It was another riddle that Jeremy had asked him, one that he could not guess. "Nothing."

Peter's glass platform moved once more, coming to rest alongside a stone ledge much like the first one he had stepped off, and he hopped lightly onto solid ground once more.

Coeus' head drooped."You are the victor." He stated sadly. "I beg of you, please, to do me one favor before you leave."

Peter raised his brows. "What?"

Coeus floated his platform to the edge near Peter. "Please kill me."

"Why would you want me to do that?" Peter asked, a shocked expression upon his face.

Coeus' face showed an expression of fear. "I have failed my King. If you do not succeed in killing him, my fate will be far worse than that of death."

Peter shook his head. "I will not kill you." He stated flatly. "I *will* kill Seth. And when I become king, I might just want you around to riddle."

Coeus' expression was indescribable. "I can only

hope for such a thing."

Peter left the ancient man with that statement, turning and forcing his way through the door behind with a thrust of the line.

- -

Memory Lane

The next room that Peter entered was large and spherical in shape, completely devoid of any decoration or structure, and lacked any discernible doors or windows; the room was a pale enamel color, giving Peter the impression of what it might be like to walk inside a giant, hollowed-out pearl. The floor just inside the threshold of the doorway was the only flat surface, and a few feet beyond that it dropped into the natural curve of the sphere.

Peter looked into the room with a dizzying feeling, like you get when you put on eyeglasses that aren't *quite* your prescription, and a thought lazily swam to the top of his mind amidst the fog: *visions.*

He tried to call the line but was overcome by—the salty, ocean air. Peter looked around, confused; he surveyed the surrounding beach, blinking, trying to determine where he was. As he did, he saw a figure in the distance, walking toward him with a steady pace; when the figure neared, he saw that it was a woman (*ding, ding, man the battle stations!*). She had long, flowing black hair, and features like that of a goddess descended from above; her shapely body, caressed by a revealing silk vesture, left Peter mesmerized as she made her way toward him with delicate, yet confident steps.

She approached until she was close enough for Peter to smell her sweet breath, which smelled of rosemary, and when she spoke, Peter was quite sure that he had never heard anything more beautiful in his lifetime.

"What is your name?" She asked, capturing Peter with every soft decibel of her angelically smooth voice.

He was silent for a long moment as he stared into her deep lavender eyes, and for a moment forgot who he was entirely, before once again regaining some semblance of his senses and opening his mouth to reply. "Peter."

She smiled, and Peter's knees felt watery. "You have beautiful eyes, Peter. They remind me of the sea; so deep, and full of tranquility."

Oh my God, I love you. Peter thought, and the beauty smiled, perhaps hearing his thought. "Thank you." He was so completely infatuated with her, that he ignored the alarm that was going off in his head, behind the eyes that could not help but look at the personification of beauty itself.

She gently took his hand. “Will you walk with me, love?”

Peter nearly fainted upon the utterance of the affectionate pet name. He was caught like a fish on a hook, so deep was he under her spell. “Into eternity.”

They walked down the beach in silence. Peter did not know how far they had gone before he realized with a start, that he had fallen deeply in love with this woman, but he knew absolutely nothing about her; not even her name.

He stopped abruptly, and she turned to him with questioning eyes. “What’s wrong?”

He looked at her with a lover’s gaze. “I do love you so, more than every grain of sand that can be found on this beach, but I don’t know your name.”

The beauty that was Peter’s love spoke with an alluringly soft, delicate voice. “I am afraid to tell you, my love.”

Peter was appalled. “Why? Why would you be afraid to tell me something so simple as your name?” (*ding, ding!! All hands!!*)

The angel spoke again, this time there was something like dread in her voice. “I am afraid that you will kill me."

Peter could not believe his ears. "Why would I kill the woman I love?"

His love hung her head, breaking his heart by the sight of it. "Because you don't love me, Peter." Before Peter could say anything, she spoke again. "I am Mnemosyne, the dream-weaver. You see the world as I want you to see it; you feel what I want you to feel."

Peter's alarm crashed against a barrier of denial with a solid *thud!* "But...I love you...I feel-" Then as quickly as they came, the feelings were gone. The world shimmered, and the beach was suddenly fading away to the room of the pearl once more; Peter found himself at the bottom of the sphere's curve, trapped by the smoothness and angle of the stone wall. He suddenly remembered everything that he had forgotten; most of all, though, he remembered where he had heard the name Mnemosyne.

He shifted an accusatory gaze at the dream-weaver, who stood a few feet away from him, still angelic in her beauty, but not quite so appealing in light of his recent flood of memory. "You tricked me!" He yelled, calling upon the line, eager to be done with the foul siren before she tried to fulfill the will of her king, and he felt raw power course through his veins (it no longer burned, only resonated with an adiabatic vibration).

She spread her hands in a gesture of submission. "If you must do so, then kill me, for to live without you would be a fate worse than death."

Peter's hold on the line faltered, then resumed its solidarity. "Spare me the adulation."

"No." She said shaking her head, her soft features were solemn. "If I wanted to continue living a lie, this hollow life, we would have stayed on the beach." She was silent a moment before continuing. "I have never *felt* before, for I am surrounded by monstrous beings, but I have seen your soul, and it's purity has humbled me."

"My soul is not pure. I am a *murderer.*" Peter stated incredulously.

Mnemosyne smiled, and it chipped a little of the ice from Peter's heart. "You kill, but you also *love*. I have seen the bond that you share with your friend, the one who lives in another world; you would give your life for him, which is a trait that I admire greatly." She waved her hand in a somewhat dismissive gesture. "These creatures that I am surrounded by are loathsome things, and their king is an abomination." She looked directly into his eyes. "If your goal is to kill the king, my love, then I will do what I can to help." She waved her hand again, and steps appeared in the curved wall of the sphere near where they were standing, leading up to a steel door (*no, Titanium. Remember the Titan?).*

Peter let the line slip just a little. "Why would you help me?"

The angelic beauty that was named Mnemosyne came near and wrapped her slender arms around Peter's waist, looking up into his eyes. "Because I want to be like you, and feel as you do; I want to be loved." Her eyes contained no hint of deception, no hint of trickery; they were only filled with adoration. Peter, through the line, could actually perceive the love in those abysmal, lavender eyes.

He let the line drop entirely, for the beauty which he perceived through it was overwhelming. He felt slightly dizzy, and the ghostly feeling of fluttering butterflies centered in his stomach. Peter beheld the woman before him, staring at him with the purity of a lover's eyes, and finally let his ancient internal walls come down; he returned her embrace with one of his own.

"Will you walk with me, love?" He whispered into her ear.

She stepped back in order to see his eyes once

more. “Into eternity.”

- -

Remember the Titan

Peter ascended the stone steps with the alien feeling of love in his heart; he held the hand of Mnemosyne, his beloved angel he had discovered in a hellish world, and together they approached the door that progressed to Titan's lair. Upon reaching the apex of the flight they tarried a bit longer, holding each other, and whispering soft words to one another.

"I have to go now, love." Peter said into the ear of his beloved. "I have to end this."

"I know," Mnemosyne whispered back, a tremble in her voice. She pulled back just enough to display lavender eyes full of hopeless devotion; their rims slowly filling with tears that would soon trail down her cheeks. "I love you."

Peter's heart shuddered; whether it merely skipped a beat or stopped entirely he could not tell. "I love you, too." He wanted to say so much more, but the words just would not come, they lay frozen in the depth of his mind and fastened in the back of his throat; it did not matter, though, for Mnemosyne could hear what his soul tried so desperately to convey, the description of feelings that neither of them had ever known existed.

"When I gaze upon you again, you shall be my king." She said with a tone of confidence that was undeniable.

Peter laid gentle hands upon the small of her back, pulling her close to him, and softly kissed her full, waiting lips; an indescribable current of electricity passed from his lips unto hers, locking their souls together, and for a single stretching moment they were no longer man and woman, but one singular entity. They withdrew reluctantly, for if they did not they would have spent the whole of eternity wrapped in each other's arms.

"Wow." Peter said dreamily.

Mnemosyne gave him a gentle push toward the door and smiled. "Go now, before I trap you in my web and refuse to let you go."

Peter smiled, still in his dreamy state as he shuffled stupefied feet toward the door. "As you wish."

Her beautiful laugh was drowned by the sound of the line's pulse, as Peter focused on the large door.

"Peter."

Peter dropped the line and turned. "Yes?"

Mnemosyne smiled her flawless smile. "You should save your strength for battle." She waved her hand, her own version of calling the line Peter supposed, and the enormous door slid aside with barely a whisper, revealing a shaft of light from the twilight sky outside.

Peter looked at his beloved, his adoration for her growing with each passing minute. "I *love* you." He said affectionately, then turned and proceeded beyond the threshold.

As Peter stepped into the soft twilight illumination he heard the door behind him slide shut; he looked behind, for a moment not wanting to continue, but then conjured a fresh image of his loved one in the mind's eye, taking comfort in those abysmal pools of lavender, and advanced onward. He had stepped onto a massive bridge that connected two spires of Seth's architecture of insanity; looking over the three-foot containing wall, he saw that he had somehow managed to ascend nearly three quarters of the capacious structure, though this fact surprised him not in the least.

Anything goes in the Mad Tower.

Peter continued across the lengthy bridge, making his way to the next spire; there was an odd hushed feeling in the air that set his nerves on edge, causing him to stop and examine his surroundings with wary eyes. He called the line, letting its vibration attune his senses; a figure far in the distance became visible to Peter's enhanced sight, waiting patiently for him as he approached the spire.

When Peter neared, he could see the figure more clearly; standing on the ledge above a large door that was similar to the one on the other end of the bridge, was a young Whooptolly with white hair, and black-feathered wings that looked as though they belonged to a fallen angel. He wore a long black coat that was fastened down the front with crisscrossing white buckles, black steel gauntlets with tapered fingers that were tipped with crimson, and gleaming white pauldrons worn atop fabric of the same crimson color; strapped to his side was a massive sword, whose blade length easily exceeded five feet.

When Peter was within earshot, he called out to the Whooptolly beyond, raising both arms in a 'y.' "What's up, T?!!"

The Whooptolly that was known as Titan regarded him with livid eyes. It raised a hand, palm outward, and released a ball of vacillating energy that Peter recognized immediately as that of the line, though it was a slightly darker color than the energy that he called upon.

Peter molded his own line, watching with amusement as the ball rocketed toward him, and at the last second before it struck and blew him off the bridge, he used crackling energy to swat it aside with all the ease of batting away a pesky moth; the ball of energy, its intended path diverted, flew about twenty yards past Peter before crashing into the containing wall and obliterating a large portion of the stone it found there.

Peter turned his head, looking at the destruction the Whooptolly line left behind, then turned back to Titan. “You missed.”

The white-haired Whooptolly let out a scream of rage, dropping down from the ledge onto light feet, and charged toward Peter with inhuman speed.

Peter hurled the line at the approaching demon, who only mimicked Peter’s first defense, swatting the energy aside; as he drew nearer he also drew his massive sword.

Oh shit. Peter thought, drawing the glass dagger.

Not good.

Titan charged forward, extending his long sword in front of him, emitting a maniacal scream.

Peter perceived a change as adrenaline caused the flow of time to shift into half frame, and watched as the honed tip of the oncoming blade came within inches of his beating heart; guided by the line, he spun in a counter-clockwise turn, deflecting the long blade away from his body by striking it with his dagger and letting momentum carry the Whooptolly past him.

Titan surprised him by not only *not* coming off-balance, but by also planting a foot (hard enough to crack the stone beneath) and bringing himself to an instant halt, swinging the sword around in a whirling counter-slash that nearly cut Peter in two; Peter jumped backward to dodge the slash, while simultaneously sending a bolt of energy at the attacker.

Titan tried to throw up a shield of the line, but was not swift enough; the bolt hit him squarely in the chest with a resounding impact, sending him skidding backward on his heels for a few feet, but not knocking him down. He looked down at the smoky point of impact on his chest with a stunned expression, then regarded Peter with an unexpected look; a congratulatory look. “A well-placed blow.”

Peter look of surprise was comical in its simplicity. “Thanks. That slash thing you did was unreal.”

The Whooptolly called Titan smiled, displaying pointed white teeth. “I first thought you unworthy to do battle with, though it seems I have underestimated your adroitness.” He sheathed his long sword and pointed to the door above which he had stood only minutes before. “If you would, please accompany me to my chambers. I will fit you with a weapon of equality to mine, and we would do battle with honor.”

Peter thought about this for a moment, not wanting to let his guard down around this powerful being; he settled on holding the line, but sheathed the dagger. “Sounds pleasantly dangerous, count me in.” He gestured to the door. “After you.”

Titan nodded, then extended his previously folded wings to their full span, beat them a few times to get the blood flowing, and took flight.

Peter watched as the black-winged warrior rose into the air, then swooped to the door previously aforementioned. *This should be interesting.* Peter thought to himself as he closed the distance between himself and the giant titanium door.

Titan waited for his opponent's approach, then threw the door open with a flick of the line, gesturing that he come inside.

Peter did so, and entered a room that contained every type of weapon that he could think of, and even a few that may have been unique to this alien world, for he had never seen the likes of them before. There were daggers and tantos, shortswords and wakaizashi, longswords and katana, sabers, broadswords, and the long-handled dai-katana; he also saw an impressive array of clubs, war staffs, hammers, battle axes, spears, bows of varying lengths, crossbows, throwing stars, and balanced throwing knives. The weapons sat perched on stands, hung on racks, and adorned shelving that covered nearly every inch of wall space; the center of the room was completely empty, and displayed intricate scuff trails from what could only be years of footwork associated with practice and the heat of battle.

Holy hell. Peter thought, studying the instruments of war.

"Do you like my collection?" Titan asked, standing a short distance away from Peter.

"It's glorious."

The Whooptolly smiled his keen smile. "Each

item was collected after I victoriously slew their owner." He walked over to a rack that was full of varying types of blades, selected a beautiful katana, its black case ornately decorated with engravings and gold trim, then displayed it in a manner where Peter could see it more clearly. "This blade belonged to the Emperor of a world called Ilthiada (ill-thee-ah-duh); it is my most prized possession, besides my friend Murasame." (mure-a-saw-me) He gestured to the massive sword at his side.

"That is quite a weapon."

Titan nodded. "I treasure it with my life." He stated affectionately, glancing down at the handle with a look that Peter could not read, then he looked back to his guest. "Have you ever been to the world called Earth?"

Peter recoiled. "That's where I'm from."

Titan smiled. "Really? I lived there for many years, linked to a man named Yojimbo; a samurai. He taught me how to fight with the blade, and how to live my life by it." He roused himself from his momentary lapse into memory and focused on Peter; holding up the katana. "I would be honored if you would have this sword, and use it to wage battle with me."

"The honor would be mine." Peter strode forth

and gently took the sword, then pulled the dagger from his belt, holding it out. "One blade for another?"

"I accept." The Whooptolly took the blade, and then placed it on a small empty set of hooks in the wall. He turned back to Peter. "Shall we begin?"

Peter hefted the katana, then drew it from its resting place, blade gleaming in the chamber's torchlight. "Let's go."

Thus the battle of lined blade ensued.

Titan drew his blade, Murasame, and hefted it with one heavily muscled arm, pointing the tip at Peter. "Make your move."

Peter immediately cross-slashed the end of the blade with katana in right hand, knocking it aside (to the left) and letting the motion pivot his body in a 180 degree turn, at the end of which he struck out with the katana's scabbard in left hand.

Titan raised a black gauntlet just in time to save his face from a crushing blow, and placed a solid kick to Peter's back, sending him shuffling. The Whooptolly then thrust his sword forward, attempting to catch Peter while he was turned and off-balance.

The blade came precariously close to one of his

kidneys before Peter spun round and deflected it (to his right) with a backhand flip of his blade, leaning his weight forward and once again bringing the scabbard up to connect with his opponent's head; Titan, whose sword hand was crossed to his left side from the deflection, had to lean his head and shoulders awkwardly to avoid the blow. As the scabbard passed over the Whooptolly's head, Peter use the force of its momentum to help him push off the ground with right foot and drive his left knee into Titan's solid chest, lifting him off the ground and driving him backward a distance of about three feet.

Titan landed on his feet (unsteadily this time), and brought a hand to his chest, an expression of pain upon his face.

Peter backpedaled a few steps to put himself out of range of Murasame, then he sheathed his katana, holding the scabbard at his left side with right hand crossed, still on it's hilt.

Titan smiled his sharp-toothed smile, impressed with Peter's move. He then contorted his face in an expression of intense concentration, and charged forth once more, sword held out to the side and prepared for a powerful slash.

Peter stood his ground as the Whooptolly

approached, waiting until the last possible moment, before bursting into motion that was guided by the all-knowing line. He thrust his sword out of the scabbard with blinding speed, sending it forth as a projectile, hilt-first, at the unsuspecting Whooptolly's face; while it still whistled through the air, Peter drove himself forward, and as the hilt collided with Titan's forehead, Peter leapt into the air, planting a substantial blow to the being's chest with leading foot, and caught the sword before it hit the ground.

Titan stumbled back a few steps, once again clutching his wounded chest. "Impressive." He said with sincerity, dusting off the front of his black coat. "You truly know how to use the line." He drew his blade across the ground in a powerful sweep, bringing up a blinding shower of rocks and dust to Peter's eyes, rendering him momentarily sightless, but not blind.

Peter pulled his katana close, holding it aside his chest with the dull side of the blade running up the side of his neck, and flexed his muscles hard, awaiting the inevitable blow that would be meant to decapitate him (though if his clairvoyance was off, and the blow was instead a thrust, he would be dead).

Clang!!

The force of the blow rocked Peter to the side, and he leapt with the momentum, rolling out of the range of any following attack, then sprang to his feet amassing a pool of the line in his mind. The relentless Whooptolly charged forward again, trying to catch Peter at a moment of weakness, but was thrown backward by a massive flat sheet of incandescent energy; his arms flailed as he flew backward, landing on his back with a heavy *thud.*

Titan slowly rolled onto his side, and rose shakily to a half-crouch, one hand on the stone floor and one hand on the hilt of his sword; he breathed laboriously, and small drips of crimson emerged from his lips, spattering onto the gray stone. “You are truly a powerful being.” He said in a unsteady voice, rising to his feet and lifting his blade, though not as easily as he had before. “Please honor me with a proper death.”

Peter decided to make a proposal. “Why should I kill someone as talented as yourself? You are an honorable being, not like the treacherous Seth, why not join my cause instead? I would have a guard such as yourself when I see him slain, and a sparring partner from which I may learn to hone my skills.”

Titan shook his head. "While indeed I would favor such a thing, my soul is bound to he who sits upon the throne, and I must give my very last breath to defend his life, as I have for many generations."

"What about the previous king? You didn't give your life for him, did you?"

A look of distaste crossed Titan's face. "I would gladly have done so, had not Seth used deceit and falsity to kill the king in his sleep, instead of facing me with honor. Because of this act, I was bound to Seth without a fight."

"Wouldn't you rather see him dead, then?"

The Whooptolly nodded. "Yes, but my soul is still bound; I cannot let you pass."

"Okay then." Peter said, stepping forth.

Titan used the last bit of his remaining strength to swing Murasame in a unsteady, upward slash.

Peter deflected the blade easily, then rapped the white-haired being on the temple with a solid blow from the katana's scabbard, dropping him to the floor, unconscious.

"Sleep tight, friend." Peter said to the fallen Titan. "When you wake, you will be bound to me."

He sheathed his new weapon, and made his way to yet another massive door, one that was second to last before coming face-to-face with the Mad King.

Oh woeful despair, I do come upon the devils lair.
I advance without fearful dismay,
Though my end may come to pass,
I may very well meet death today.

- -

Like a Fox, Man

The door upon which Peter approached slid aside with but a passing gesture, for the line was with him. He entered with absolute caution, for he approached the den of the beast, and did not want to be caught unwary; the room he entered was a vast library, filled with countless shelves and bookcases that stretched beyond perception, each heavily weighted by numerous volumes.

Peter gazed at the room in awe as he picked his way through the shelves; if all the books on earth had been compiled into one space, it would still have been rivaled by the Whooptolly literature, such was its magnitude. He reached out to a nearby shelf and plucked a sizable volume from it, opening it to a random page (pg. 51).

"Ab incunabulis absit invidia, amicus humani—"

Peter drew his eyes from the unintelligible words,

calling a flow of the line into his thoughts, then looked back to the page.

"Ab incunabulis (from infancy) absit invidia (let there be no ill will), amicus humani generis (friend of the human race), corruptio optimi pessima (for corruption of the best is the worst of all). Humanum est errare (to err is human), finem respice (but consider the end); ignorantia juris neminem excusat (ignorance of the law excuses no one)."

Wow. Peter thought, placing the book back on the shelf and continuing his trek through the maze of knowledge.

He passed between two massive shelves full of books, and came into a rounded clearing, beyond which he could see the entrance to Seth's chamber. What he saw in the center of the clearing drew his thoughts from the oncoming battle with Seth, such was the oddity of the sight.

There in the center of the clearing stood a creature with the body of a man, dressed in an ornate robe of crimson, with long pointed fingernails that were kept meticulously clean, and the head of a red fox; its passive eyes seethed with a somber intelligence that was undeniably benign.

Peter could sense an immense power within the being, one that far surpassed that of Titan and himself; it was as if the fox-man could not only draw from the line, but was a *part* of the line itself.

The oddity stood next to an altar of blackened Whooptolly glass, which was adorned with many candles of the same color that circled a thick leather tome. The tome was decorated with characters and hieroglyphs that were foreign to Peter's eyes, and secured with a thick metal clasp that displayed an odd-shaped keyhole.

The creature regarded Peter with it's intelligent eyes, and spoke in a resounding voice that seemed to come from many directions at once. "Hello Peter."

Peter had at this point in time learned to let unexpected occurrences, such as how the *hell* a half-man, half-fox creature from a parallel world could *possibly* know his name, just roll off him. "Hey there, foxy. What's crackin'?"

The fox-man surprised him by saying, "Not much, skinny. Just chillin' here in wonderland, babysittin' this big-ass book."

Peter allowed his jaw to drop slightly; all rolling aside, he wasn't expecting that.

The fox-man gave a little smile. "I guess you could say that I'm a *worldly* fellow."

Peter regained his composure, though with a bit of difficulty. "Whom may I ask are you, friend? And what is your purpose here in this tower of madness?"

The fox-man raised a hand to chest, adding a regal quality to his introduction. "I am Custos Morum (coos-tose' more-rum), Sentient of the line and guardian of the Tome."

Peter pointed at the large book. "That? What is it?"

Custos assumed the voice of a professor giving lecture. "The Tome is the map of the multi-verse, *ab uno disce omnes*, and contains the glyphs of all the worlds."

"I see. Do you serve the Mad King? Do you let him peer into its pages?"

The Sentient shook his head. "No. I am subject to nothing save the line."

Peter furrowed his brows. "The Mad King allows your presence in the castle?"

"He has no choice."

Oh. Peter thought. "If I were to tell you that my purpose in coming to this world was to kill the king, would you then consider me an enemy?"

The fox-man regarded him with bewildered eyes.

"Why should I do such a thing as that? It's your

prerogative to do as you will, so long as you bother not the Tome of the Worlds." The creature winked. "Though if you do succeed in your task, I might be willing to let *you* have a peek."

"Really?" Peter asked. "I'd love to. May I ask why you'd let one such as me, who has already stated intent to slay another being, behold something as precious as the Tome?"

Custos shrugged. "I see your line, and it is bright; worthy of sight. Plus, I like you. You have funny thoughts."

Peter nodded. "Okay then, I'll hold you to that. See you later, fox-man."

"Late."

What an odd creature. Peter thought to himself as he turned to approach the large, jewel-encrusted door that was the entrance to the bloody king Seth's lair. *Good guy, though.*

Peter stood in front of the last door he would enter as an ordinary man, for when he passed through the next, he would not be a man, but a *king.*

Here I stand before the door,
The trail behind me
Painted with madness and gore.
Across the threshold beyond,

Sits the Mad King Seth
Pale architect of death's sweet song.

- -

Throne of Death

The door to hell was encrusted with jewels of a crimson color, blood rubies if you will, and etched with engravings that depicted the submission of, and the gruesome torture of the seafaring people that once called this world home. Above the depictions of cruelty, overlooking the scene, was the bust of a sharp-toothed lion's head in mid-roar (bringing to mind the MGM logo screen on old movies), sculpted from a large single piece of gold.

Peter stared upon the bust of the lion with amusement, for he could not help but find humor in Seth's attempt at imagery. The king may have thought that the image of nature's own king upon his royal door was a majestic thing, but Peter looked upon the sculpture with another image in mind. To hide behind his tower, and all the guardians within, showed a hint of Seth's true underlying character; in Peter's mind, the bust was a depiction of that very same character.

The cowardly lion.

"How fitting."

Peter reached out to try the door, but drew his hand back again when the lion began to speak.

"Open not this door, mortal one, for beyond it lies the chamber of the Dark King." The statue warned with a stentorian voice.

Peter addressed the lion in a mocking tone. "Fear not, my twenty-four carat amigo, for I am a good friend of your king Seth, and I do believe he is expecting me."

"The king of which you speak does not have friends." The bust replied in its booming, baritone voice. "He is a bellicose being, and has taken no audience in some time; all those who have entered this chamber in recent days have not emerged among the living, if at all. So I say to you, beware this place. Turn aside and flee while you can still do so."

"Yeah, yeah. Abandon hope all ye who enter, and all that jazz. I'll take my chances."

"I'm afraid I cannot let you pass."

Peter brought his face close to the animated sculpture, looking at it with a cold gaze, and whispered softly. "If you don't open up, I'm gonna rip you off this frame and turn you into a overpriced doorknob."

There was a sharp *click* as the door's internal lock mechanism released.

"That's what I thought." Peter pushed the door open, revealing a candlelit throne room. Following his initial steps past the threshold and into the room, the door closed behind; he progressed into the monolithic chamber amidst a flood of memories, eyes fixed upon the maddened king with each fateful step taken.

Seth sat upon his throne of death; the king of this woeful land of demons. Corpses high in their stage of rotting littered the floors around the throne, as if biding their time until they too could serve as stone and mortar for the ever-growing royal seat. Thirteen levels of human skulls, held together with cement, formed the steps leading to the throne, and the handrails alongside were adorned with severed heads mounted on sharp spikes, each facing inward, as if to witness the Mad King in his glory as he climbed or descended the cruel steps. The high-backed seat itself was also made of human skulls, with a thick mat of hair to serve as a cushion; black candles sat upon each arm of the throne, fastened in place by dripping wax that reminded Peter of the viscous fluid that ran in the Sentry's veins, and they emitted a soft glow upon Seth that gave his pale face a sinister look.

Peter stopped just short of the last step that lead to the throne, and then shook a finger at the king. "You've been a busy little devil, haven't you?"

Seth smiled. "Petey, m'boy." He said in a jovial voice. "What an unpleasant surprise. I thought for sure you'd be dead by now."

Peter shook his head. "Years in a coffin being eaten by worms just doesn't appeal to me, I guess. I get claustrophobic."

"How *did* you manage to get past Titan? He was my best."

Peter shrugged. "I guess his sword was too short."

Seth slammed the arm of his grotesque throne with a clenched fist, emitting a snake-like hiss and baring teeth that resembled that of a great white shark. "Don't play with me, Petey! The time for humor has passed; I am king and you will treat me as so!"

Peter laughed. "You are the king of nothingness; a weak ruler that hides behind hate and violence, feeding on the fear of those you victimize, and forever submitting to blind feral instinct."

Seth leapt to his feet, shaking with rage. "Shut

your mouth, knave! I will not be spoken to in such a manner by a mere mortal!"

"I will speak as I please, for I bow to no one!"

Seth's shriek of rage resounded throughout the room. "Then you can die!!" Pure crimson flame shot forth from one of his outstretched hands in a steady stream and engulfed Peter, turning him into a human torch. The king cackled with glee as he raised his remaining hand to add a second stream of liquid fire. "We don't need no water! Let the motherfucker burn!" He screamed over the thunder of the burning inferno.

A concentrated burst of linear energy cut through the crimson flames and struck the king in mid-cackle, sending him hurtling backward though the air and into the throne, which gave way to the weight and sheer velocity of the flying Seth, and he landed amongst the cadavers and bone dust that littered the floor beyond.

Peter emerged from the smoke unscathed by the unholy flames, and released the line. "Burn motherfucker, burn." He said impassively.

"Petey," Seth groaned from the floor behind the decimated throne. "You *suck!*" He coughed, then rose to his feet.

"Come now mighty king," Peter said, drawing his

katana from its scabbard. "Let us be finished with this business of ours, for I grow weary of your foul essence."

"Petey, why must we fight?" Seth asked in a bargaining tone, holding out his hands in a gesture of submission. "Why, when we could be so much more if we struck an alliance? Just think of it: we could Shear through all the worlds, taking them one by one, until we were the rulers of all the multi-verse. You and I, unstoppable, with the worlds at our fingertips." Seth smiled his keen smile, Mephistopheles' smile. "What would you say to that?"

Peter gave Seth a look that wiped the smile right off his face. "I would say that you took out a hefty loan on your ass the moment you threatened Jeremy, you pale fuck, and it's high-time to pay the fine."

Seth stepped around the remains of the throne, and unsheathed two glass daggers that were identical to that which Peter had left in Titan's chamber. "So you desire power, is that it? You want the throne?" Seth asked, a touch of desperation in his voice.

Peter shook his head. "Nope. I could care less about being king, but it would be hard."

"Then *why*?"

Peter shrugged. "I dunno. I guess there's just something about you that pisses me off."

Seth flung a ball of flame at Peter, who batted it aside like a crumpled paper. "Dammit Petey, why don't you just *leave*?" He tried to dash toward a nearby exit.

"We have a score to settle, you coward!" Peter yelled, and moved into the path of Seth's weak attempt at escape. "You *will* face me."

Seth tried to plead once more. "Petey, I'll make you *king*. I'll renounce my throne and leave this world, and yours, and you'll never see me again. Just let me go."

Peter raised his katana into mid-stance. "Defend yourself, old friend."

A look of utter hopelessness swept across Seth's pallid features and he raised his twin daggers. "I guess there's no changing this, then."

"Nope."

"So be it. Make your move."

Peter obliged. He rushed forward, bringing the katana up in a strong upward slash, and his blade met glass with bright sound. He unleashed a rapid fusillade of blows, each met and deflected by Seth's blinding daggers, until he ceased his flow with a backward leap. He rushed forward once more, bringing the sword in a downward slash; when the blade rebounded, he spun around to attack from the other side, but was met again by glass blade. A swift kick sent Peter stumbling.

He stared at Seth (whose eyes had turned a solid black) with a bewildered look.

Seth smiled with pointed teeth, and regarded him with inhuman eyes of darkness. “Surely you didn’t think this was going to be *easy*, did you?” He leapt forward with confident triumph, daggers arcing precariously toward his target’s unprotected throat; Peter let the facade of confusion fall away, and chuckling, side-stepped the whistling blades, giving a twirl of his katana as the king passed.

A scream of surprised pain filled the air as the pinkie from Seth’s right hand was ablated, and a spray of blackened blood joined the two in their flight. Seth dropped his blades and clutched his wounded hand, screaming in agony.

“Yeah.” Peter said. “Actually, I did.” He motioned to the daggers. “Arm yourself.”

Seth did as he was told, biting back still another scream, with difficulty; his right hand had started to swell, and the fingers didn’t grasp so well without their last digit. His breathing was ragged, for he had never felt as much pain as he felt presently, and was not very tolerant of it.

Suddenly the door to the main hall opened, emitting three figures: Mnemosyne, Coeus, and Titan. Peter gave a wary glance to Titan, hand ready on the hilt of his katana, but Titan shook his head and gave a twirling gesture with the fingers of his right hand. *Continue.*

Seth looked at the three figures with shocked dismay. "But I thought..."

"You are not the great king that you believe yourself to be." Coeus stated, stepping forward from the group. "Long have you ruled my over my people with fear and bloodshed. This man has come to us with an offer of peace. *Peace.*" The man shook his head. "By the gods, I would gladly pledge my life to this outworlder for just one more taste of that sweetness."

"You are traitorous cowards!! All of you!!" Seth screamed. "I am your king!! You will obey me!! Kill this man!!"

"You are no king of mine." Titan said, stepping forward to stand beside Coeus. "You are a dishonorable creature, and a coward yourself for slaying the good king Verucian in his sleep. Your atonement is no longer your own choice."

"And you, Mnemosyne?" Seth asked. "What is your reason for betrayal?"

The siren stepped forward to be among the others. "This man possesses something that is more powerful than anything I've encountered in my centuries of living."

"Which is?"

Mnemosyne smiled. "Love."

Seth shook his head. "You've all lost your minds. This is unacceptable." He flipped the dagger in his good hand and caught it by the blade, then threw it toward the rebels; while it still spun in mid-air, with the wounded opposite hand he cast a fiery orb that shattered the blade, sending several large shards of the fragmented glass spraying in a cloud of shrapnel.

Peter slashed with his blade just as another burst of crimson began to leave Seth's fingertips, and the emitted arterial spray was vaporized in the wake of the heat; the pinkiless hand plopped down onto the floor, cauterized. Seth's resulting howl was silenced as Peter whirled, swinging his katana with all his might, and cleaved through the neck of the being that had been his friend for nearly thirteen years, decapitating him.

Seth's head hit the floor and bounced, coming to

rest at the bottom step of the broken throne, and his eyes rolled to regard Peter. "There are many worlds, Petey m'boy, and I live in them all." The disembodied head stated, blood painting pale lips crimson. "I...live...in...them...all..." The light in Seth's eyes then dimmed, and he spoke no more.

Peter stared at his fallen nemesis for a long moment that was gravid with emotion, then he looked behind, and his heart dropped. The shrapnel from the glass dagger had not spread very far, for Titan and Coeus suffered only minimal scratches and glass splinters, but Mnemosyne had not been so fortunate.

Peter dropped his katana and rushed to the side of his fallen beloved and knelt; a thin piece of the glass dagger had broken off and lodged into the side of her throat, and she bled profusely from the wound. He reached for the glass shard, intending to remove it in a moment of unthinking panic, then stopped himself, remembering something he had seen on a rescue program years before. A similar situation had occurred where a victim had been stabbed in the neck by a mugger, and someone removed the knife from the wound at the scene; the victim bled to death in a matter of minutes.

He cast a desperate look to the two onlookers.

"Do something! She's dying!!"

Titan gave him a confused look. "What would you have me do?"

Peter nearly leapt up and tore the bastard's head off. "Heal her!! Get me a band aid!! Do *something* other than just standing there with your thumb up your ass!!"

"There's nothing that can be done." Coeus said in a level voice.

I'm gonna kill this sonuvabitch. Peter thought, starting to rise.

"My...love." Mnemosyne said in a strained voice that was thick with blood, causing Peter to forget all else and return to her side.

"Yes, my love. What is it?" Peter asked, his breath hitched in his chest, an oppressive weight, and tears stung his eyes as they made trails down his bloodstained cheek.

Mnemosyne struggled to summon the breath to speak. "Fear...not...my...sweet." Her chest shuddered, and she exhaled a long breath...but her chest did not rise again.

Peter's body shook. He stared at his love with glistening eyes, and his soul began to weep; he issued a long, painful scream of despair, for he had lost love while it was still so new. The tears burned with a hollow bitterness, and they fell upon the body of his still beloved. As he held her in his arms, her color began to fade, the soft, warm tone of her smooth angelic skin becoming rough and gray; at the end of the transformation, she collapsed in upon herself, and all that remained was a pile of ashes, with a single thin shard of black glass within.

With tears in his eyes and hopelessness in his heart, Peter reached into the pile, plucking the shard free; he closed his eyes and held it to his chest, sobbing.

“My king.”

Peter opened his eyes, and looked upon the blurred speaker.

Titan regarded him with eyes that were filled with awe. “Never before have I seen this thing, what you call love, and it has humbled me, my lord.”

“Aye.” Coeus agreed. “And I as well.”

“With that being said,” Titan started, “I must insist: there is no reason to fret. That is what the one you love hath tried to tell thee.”

“How can you sit there and tell me that?” Peter asked. “She’s dead!! She turned to *ashes*.”

Coeus nodded. “That is true, but is there not another creature that turns to ashes when it dies?”

Peter did not understand, so blinded was he by

pain and grief."What are you *talking* about?"

"Have you ever heard of a creature called the *phoenix*?"

Understanding dawned on Peter, clearing the fog that clouded his mind. "You mean she will be reincarnated?" Peter asked, hope flooding back into his deadened heart.

The two men nodded.

"Thus from the ashes shall she be reborn, to live aside you forever, and warm you forevermore." Coeus said in a poetic manner, smiling.

Peter felt a soft breeze upon his cheek, and he once again turned to the ashes that lay upon the floor; he watched as the ashes began to swirl, like a foot-tall tornado, and then grow in size. He stepped back as the tornado grew, and a silhouette began to take shape; Peter watched as the ashes grew legs, then hips, then shoulders, and then a face. When the winds of change calmed, his beloved stood before him once more, angelic in her nakedness, smiling as though she had not been ashes only a moment before.

Peter stared at her, enamored of her simplistic beauty, and then he went to her, wrapping his arms around her. "I thought you were dead. Oh god, I thought you were dead."

She held him as tightly as he needed her to. “I told you not to fear, love, and I would *never* lie to you.”

“I love you.”

Peter’s angel gently pulled away from his fierce embrace, smiling. “And I you.”

Out of the corner of his eye, Peter watched Titan and Coeus drop to kneel, and when he regarded them, they spoke in unison. “Long live the king!! Long live king Peter!! May he bring peace among us!!”

Peter nodded. “I am honored, and will do my best. But for now, I ask that you leave me with my queen, brothers, for we have much to discuss.”

They obliged, and as the two proceeded to the chamber’s exit, Mnemosyne looked into Peter’s eyes with longing. “Long live the king.”

- -

Epilogue

On a distant plane of existence, far beyond the world of the sea, there lay a world of jagged rock and broken desert, blanketed by an eternal night. Deep in the heart of this desolate world, there lay a cave, full of the bones of creatures that were unfortunate enough to stray within, searching for shelter from the relentless desert storms.

Within the recesses of the cave, devoid of all light, there lurked a man with black hair, gnawing on the bones of his latest kill. The man (but not really a man, more like demon) smiled a bemused smile, stray pieces of meat stuck in the crevices of his jagged teeth.

"There are many worlds..." The man said, cackling with madness. "And I live in them all!!"

Long live the king.

Lightning Source UK Ltd.
Milton Keynes UK
UKOW02f2325260716

279326UK00001B/38/P

9 781607 034551